# *not so best wishes*

## WARTS & CLAWS INC BOOK 2

### CLIO EVANS

"I live by one rule: No office romances. No way. Very messy.
Inappropriate. No. But, I live by another rule: Just do it...
Nike." — Michael Scott, The Office

# *warning!*

# just another manticore monday

## LORA

I rushed through the front lobby, cussing under my breath as I badged through the security gate and went straight to the elevator.

This morning had been shit. Every single thing that could go wrong on a Monday morning had gone wrong.

My dryer had gone out, so my clothes were slightly damp. I'd hit every red light on my drive and spilled my iced latte on my front seat. If I didn't know any better, I would say that someone had cursed me— but cursing a demon was damn near impossible.

The elevator doors slid open, and I stepped in, melting against the wall. They were about to close, but a foot parted them, and someone stepped in.

Damn it. I really wanted to be alone right now.

I looked up at them and realized they were a witch. One I had never seen before.

Heat rose in my cheeks. They exuded the type of sexual energy I would want to climb them for.

They wore a navy blue suit with a black tie and undershirt, their Oxfords glossy in the yellow lighting. Their hair was short and jet black, eyes fully black with violet irises. A silver earring glinted in their right ear as they chose their spot in the elevator.

There was a hum of magic bleeding from them, an aura of energy that made me both nervous and want to step closer.

Damn it. It was too early to be in the elevator with someone this pretty.

I looked down at my nails, pretending to check out the glossy black paint.

Most creatures thought of me as less of a monster because I was part fae and part demon. I leaned more into my demonic side, but I had a dainty appearance that some mistook for 'not monster enough'. They didn't know I could get into their minds if I wanted. I was very good at luring those around me into my circle so I could rip off their heads if I desired.

If I ever started singing some of the hymns I knew from my family, hell would rip open just for me.

They barely spared me a glance, and I straightened, happy to ignore them. Today was not the day for me, and I didn't want to fight with this witch.

Especially after the last few weeks.

About three weeks ago, the company I worked for merged with another. Claws Inc. became Warts & Claws Inc., and the first week had been hell. I dealt with a crazy HR rep that tried to break into my mind, while my coworker's lives had been threatened.

The good news was the last week had settled down.

Monsters and witches were working well enough, and the boss upstairs was at least present.

The elevator doors were about to shut again when a pair of claws parted them.

"For fuck's sake," I hissed.

The claws belonged to none other than Mich, the manticore I shared a desk with. He stepped in and gave me a little smile and a shrug. "Morning. You look..."

"Don't fucking say anything," I hissed.

That earned a side look from the witch that had taken to the opposite side from us. I found myself staring for a few moments, unable to look away.

Their gaze slid over me, their lips curling into a little smile.

Fuck.

I looked away, trying to purge my thoughts before I started thinking about how attractive they were.

Mich leaned forward and mashed the button, letting out a sigh. His shoulders were tense, his mane a little frazzled. His wings were pulled tight, his bulky muscles rippling under his blazer.

I always liked looking at him when he wasn't paying attention. His fur was the color of honey, and I wished I could see him in his entire monster form. Even though he let his wings out sometimes, and occasionally his scorpion tail— in the office, he usually remained closed off to us all.

Although, slowly but surely, he was talking to me more.

Manticores were known to be sexy as fuck. A part of me wanted to find out just how true that was, but there was a stone wall between work and his personal life.

If anything, it made me more curious about who he really was.

"Traffic was a bitch this morning, and I don't know

how I feel about coming back. Every Monday is another day that makes me wonder if I need this job," he grumbled.

I gave a little nod, relaxing some. "It's been crazy, but it does pay well."

"We should try to get raises considering," Mich chuckled.

The witch cleared their throat, and we both looked at them. Mich narrowed his eyes on them and then looked down at me, arching a furry brow.

The look was, 'do you know this witch?'

I shook my head and shrugged, keeping my mouth shut, trying not to look too long at Mich.

Trying not to look back at the witch.

God damn, I was entirely too thirsty this morning.

"Well, even if we're late, I doubt Inferna will care," Mich said with a shrug.

Maybe. Inferna was a good boss and had saved our asses recently. I would never forget her banning the HR psycho from the office.

"Art doesn't seem too bad either," I sighed.

"Well, you know how I feel about witches sometimes," Mich said, not giving two shits that there was one in the elevator. "Well, particularly rude ones. But I suppose I feel that way about everyone."

I gave the witch an apologetic look, but they were staring straight ahead. They were thinking hard about something, and I wondered what it was.

Mich let out a little chuckle as the elevator stopped, delivering us to the office. He stepped to the side, giving me a slight nod.

"Ladies first," he said.

I was about to walk by when the witch moved past us.

Mich released a very dark growl and started to reach for them, but I pulled him back.

"It's fine," I said softly, holding on to his burly arm.

"What the fuck is their problem?" Mich sneered.

"Come on," I said, hooking my arm with his and dragging him forward.

I may have been tiny compared to him, but I was still a strong little monster. Mich growled again, but ultimately I pulled him down the hall and through the office doors.

"Morning, Lora," a sweet voice called.

I paused, seeing Anne sitting at her desk. She had the serpents around her head pulled back today, her eyes dusted with gold eyeshadow. She was wearing a dark green top that looked great on her.

She did the business look in a very sexy manner, which I admired even though that was not my style.

She was quickly becoming a good friend of mine, someone I wouldn't mind hanging out with outside of work. We'd bonded since that fucking HR bitch had caused so much trouble.

"Morning, Anne," I said, winking at her.

She flashed her fangs in a grin, arching her brow at the way I led Mich through the office.

I glanced at the clock as we went to our desks, letting out a sigh of relief as we made it. Ten minutes late, but no one really seemed to care.

Calen was already sitting in his spot and gave us a sweet smile. "I was starting to get worried I was working alone today."

Mich grunted, shrugging my arm off and moving to his seat. He raked his claws through his mane, rolling his shoulders. "Almost ate a witch, but Lora stopped me."

"Oh?" Calen asked, his eyes widening.

"Don't mind him, Calen," I said, smiling back at him. "There was just an asshole in the elevator. Not sure who they are."

"Oh," Calen said. "One of the witches here?"

"Someone new," Mich grunted. "Better not be a new hire, or I will turn their fancy suit into fucking napkins for the cafeteria."

I let out a little laugh and then set my bag down, settling into my chair. I wore a black dress with a high neck lace eyelet collar, sheer tights, and my clunky platform boots that made me look like a goth doll. Just how I liked it, even though my clothing was still drying from this morning. I smelled like damp dryer sheets and coffee.

With a small sigh, I mentally collected myself and started my computer. At least I was here and somewhat on time.

I had successfully forgotten about everything that happened recently over the weekend, but now I was here again. Anxiety crept through me, but I reminded myself that the HR rep wasn't here. It had been some time, and things had settled down.

It was almost a normal work environment if you ignored that everyone was a creature and that sometimes things happened— like Anne accidentally biting one of the werewolf boys or one of the witches setting one of the demons on fire because they sneezed really hard.

Or the fact that our new HR agent had been fucking evil. Alice had been a very strong witch. Strong enough to break through the mental shields I had up.

I would need to deal with that emotions at some point, but I wasn't quite ready. Instead, I packed them into a neat little box and shoved them into the dark corner of my mind.

The place where I let trauma wilt and would only deal with it when my therapist made me.

My therapist was a genie that had been freed by his mate. Sometimes his words were more like riddles, but he still helped. Hell, every monster needed therapy at this point.

A lot of the monsters here had been around for ages and were trying to fit into a modern world. One where we could have apps that would filter out our monster qualities, and one where humans and monsters might actually fall in love. One where it wasn't so uncommon to see a werewolf witch, a vampire centaur, or a daytime sleep paralysis demon.

"You look nice today," Calen said, giving me another sweet smile.

"Thanks, Calen," I said, grinning. "How was your weekend?"

"Well, we went to Inferna's godfather's coffee shop. It was interesting. He matches monsters with humans."

"Interesting indeed," I said, frowning a little. "Well, there are apps for that now."

Calen and I both grinned. Apps that needed work.

"I think he does better than the apps, but yes. He was nice enough."

"Good!" I said cheerfully. "I'm happy to hear that."

"What did you do this weekend?"

I blanked for a moment. What did I do this weekend? Aside from crocheting demon-summoning circle floor mats and drinking ghost reaper chai tea?

Literally nothing.

"I worked on some stuff," I said vaguely.

There was nothing wrong with having zero social life outside of work. Right?

"Is the big boss guy in?" I asked, redirecting him.

"Yeah," Calen said, looking out across the office. "Inferna and Art are with him upstairs."

Upstairs. We had apparently acquired a whole other floor, but it was only for Inferna and Alex. I didn't care, though. I liked sitting with Calen.

In fact, I really never had issues with witches until recently. The demons in my family had married into some covens and vice versa.

The monsters in this area who had problems with witches, in particular, were the same monsters who had dealt with whatever fight happened nearby years ago.

The same could be said for vampires.

I didn't like that the world of monsters had divisions. Witches and vampires seemed to stick together. Demons really loved their fae creatures. The Naga and Basilisk families had a whole network and world within worlds.

Still, humans were slowly getting more and more exposed to our kind, which was why I worked at this office and for this company. I liked working on the app that helped monsters find love, even if it was similar to catfishing at first.

I felt eyes on me and looked up, meeting Mich's gaze. He held it for a moment, and my heart skipped a beat.

There was something about him I found comforting, even though he was very clearly off-limits in general. He didn't interact with many in the office, and after all the bullshit with Hazard betraying everyone, I wasn't sure he would improve.

Still, he was watching me like he wanted to devour me.

I cocked my head, and he blinked, clearing his throat.

Everyone was chatting around at their different desks, some conversations more hushed than others. Still, the low thrum of white noise didn't muffle his soft little growl.

Fuck. I wanted him to do that in my ear.

Maybe I needed to go out and get laid. It had been far too long since I'd fucked someone.

I could go to one of the clubs after work. At least then, I could fulfill the voyeur part of me. I wouldn't mind watching a human get ravaged by tentacles or a mage whipped by her Dom.

Maybe Anne would go with me.

Even though I mostly stayed home, occasionally, I would throw caution to the wind and go somewhere. The only worry I ever had was my ex, but he was on the other side of the country and had no clue where I'd gone.

Maybe Mich would go with me...

Mich suddenly stood up, bumping our tables. He stood still for a moment and then scowled.

"I'm going to get breakfast. I might also take a break and shift for a few minutes. I feel itchy. But I'll bring you something to eat. If someone is getting in trouble for not working, it can be me," he grumbled.

"Oh," I said, frowning. "Don't worry about me, Mich. If you need to go shift, take care of yourself."

"I'm getting you breakfast."

I blinked, surprised by his bluntness. "Okay then. Thanks."

Mich ignored me, leaving the office.

I watched him go. When he was in the office, he looked more like a lion than a manticore, but I knew he had wings, dragon spikes, and a scorpion tail too.

Calen raised a brow. "Is he okay?"

"I think so?" I frowned, watching him until he disappeared out of sight.

"I know holding a half-shifted form has to be difficult,"

Calen said. "Inferna does well with her wings, but I know she needs good shoulder rubs after work."

I fought a little smile, a somewhat jealous one. I wanted someone to rub my back at the end of the day.

I'd had someone to go home to once upon a time, but they only stabbed me in the back.

"You have no idea," I said, letting out a helpless laugh.

Even now, my shoulders ached from holding in my wings. I kept them in, though, so I didn't draw any attention or knock things over.

In fact, I kept a lot of things to myself.

Calen gave me another kind smile, and then the two of us both sighed, starting our work for the day.

# *confidential*

## CINDER

"So you're the new HR rep," the succubus said, studying me as if I were a specimen on a dish.

There were two witches here too, but neither seemed to be as irritated by my presence as she was. The four of us were seated in a nice office, but the vanilla walls were bare, and there were boxes of office supplies still being unpacked.

The window showed us a nice view of the building across the street, and that was about it.

I might have been offended, but if they knew why I was here, they would have a right to be angry. Of course, all of the details I had about how Alice had failed made Inferna's attitude toward me understandable.

"Cinder," Alex said, clearing his throat. "It's been three weeks, but the first week was a disaster."

Alex was the big boss. The one I had to be the most aware of. I had never met the monster pulling all the strings, but I knew they despised Alex.

"So I heard," I said. "I'm not entirely sure of the details, but I'm here to help. It shouldn't have taken this long to get me out here."

When I wanted to woo others, I could. Easily. It was second nature to be nice, charming, and everything they wanted in an HR rep.

It was easy, given that I could read auras. I could see the colors of someone's mood and how they interacted with others.

My magic had always had its quirks, but the constant reading of auras was one I enjoyed.

I was here on the same mission as Alice had been.

It wasn't that I liked what I did, but I had no choice. My sister was an omega witch, and the only reason she hadn't been taken yet was that I was willing to infiltrate Warts & Claws Inc. What they were using that magic for, I wasn't sure. I was kept in the dark on a lot of details. But I knew that I could be in trouble if I didn't do exactly as they wanted.

Alex had no fucking clue how deep the corruption ran. Claude was just the tip of the iceberg.

I thought about the cute pixie in the elevator and the manticore at her side.

They had no idea either, making me feel guilty for what I was here to do.

Still, I had no choice. Not yet, anyway.

"We can cover the details," Alex said. "I made some decisions as far as leadership goes. Also, Inferna, he will need—"

"They will need. I use they and them as my pronouns," I said, interrupting Alex.

Alex paused thoughtfully and then nodded. "Apologies.

They will need a desk for their things. Also, my pronouns are he/him."

"Mine are she and her," Infena said, offering me a softer smile, "although I don't mind they or them." Inferna looked over at Art, arching a brow. "I guess we could seat them where Hazard was for the time being. We can figure out office space later."

"Perhaps," Art said. "Also, he or him. Thank you. We should add pronouns to our hiring sheets. And yes, Hazard's desk can work temporarily."

I nodded, forcing myself to relax at the mention of Hazard.

Hazard had been one of the spies here, but he was now doing other things since Alice had been discovered. And by other things, I wasn't sure where he had gone.

He was someone I didn't want to interact with.

"That's a good idea. I'm surprised you haven't already, but I know the company has undergone a drastic change," I said.

"Yes, in the last month," Inferna sighed. "We need therapy available for our employees. We need to make sure everyone is okay after everything that happened. So, I think the best thing you can do for now is work alongside everyone and get to know them. Seeing as our corporate boss is in the building, I'm sure he can get the ball rolling with what everyone needs. If we have any issues that come up, we can all handle them accordingly. Also, just to be transparent, Art, Calen, and I are all in a relationship."

That explained the auras between the two of them.

"Good to know," I said, smirking. "I suppose it goes without saying, but PDA should be kept to a minimum."

"Oh, they save that for when they're alone in the elevator," Alex chuckled. "It should also be known that everything the four of us discuss is to be kept confidential. We are unsure exactly what the motives were of the creatures involved in the incidents with Claude and Alice. But I was imprisoned in their hold for a bit in none other than the basement of the building. It seems like there hasn't been any activity, and we also hired some of the witches that needed a job while they sort everything out. I'm just glad that these two were able to get me out, even if they didn't realize I was down there."

I widened my eyes, feigning shock. "I know that it can be complicated when monsters run businesses. All of the outside factors to our world come crashing in."

"Indeed," Alex said, studying me.

The way he watched me was entirely more jarring than anyone else. Surely he didn't know I was here on a mission? And what if he did?

The boss had been clear about my purpose under the sickly sweet guise of threat through one of his servants. The first agent, Alice, had failed, murdered no less.

Claude had failed too.

The goal was to take any omega witches that appeared here and to tear down the three in front of me. But first, I had to win them over.

I ignored the feeling I had rooted in my gut, reminding myself about my sister.

Ember was safe because of me.

"The witches that survived will be starting soon," Alex said. "They will need a place to work while they go through healing from being captured and their magic used. I would like for you to keep a close eye on them and to be a healthy resource."

"Lora needs to be talked to as well," Inferna said, tapping the tips of her nails on her pant leg. "Alice did some damage. She at least needs to be checked on. I'm not sure how willing she will be to share what happened."

"I'm glad Alice is gone," Art growled, his eyes flashing with fury for a moment.

"I'm here to help," I said.

Was it possible to say something that was both the truth and a lie?

I did want to help those that were hurt, even though I knew I was only helping the source of the problems. If I were able to break out of this cycle, I would.

But Ember was in danger.

I hated what I had to do to keep us both safe, but it was necessary.

"Excellent. Well, we need to get on to other matters. Art will show you to your temporary desk. You'll be at Mich, Lora, and Calen's desk," Alex said. "If you have any issues, let Art know. If you need anything further, then escalate it up to Inferna and then myself. Inferna and I are going to be going over contracts amidst other things to do with her new position and the future of this company. Whatever the enemy wants to do, they will not succeed. I will see to it. And, at the end of the day, we are simply here to build an app that will improve the lives of creatures."

Spoken like a true boss. I nodded, holding out my hand. Alex shook it, and then all of us rose.

"Come on," Art said. "I'll show you to your desk."

I followed Art out of the office to the elevators. His aura darkened some, changing from the vibrant blue it had been around Inferna to a stormy gray. We stepped in, and he hit the button, letting out a sigh.

"Witch to witch," he said, looking directly at me. "I will destroy you if you show any of the signs that Alice had. My mate was almost killed. I don't know how HR reps are selected or how deep this trouble goes, but if you know anything, you should just tell us."

"I don't," I lied, looking at him.

We stared at each other for a moment, and then he pressed his lips together. "So be it. Good luck. You have some work ahead of you to win over the office. Alice did a lot of damage in the short time she was here, and I don't think it's amiss for everyone to doubt you will be better."

The elevator doors slid open, and I was led to the office, passing by the receptionist. Her eyes landed on me, narrowing.

In fact, everyone in the office paused in chatting to steal glances at me as I followed behind Art.

He led me to four desks in the corner of the room, nestled towards the back by a window that at least allowed some natural light in. There was a witch in a button-down wearing glasses and that pixie girl I had seen in the elevator.

I wished I could see her wings. She was already gorgeous as she was, her piercings glinting in the sunlight. I couldn't help but wonder if her wings were like glass or if they were solid.

I had a thing for wings.

Fuck, I had a thing for goth pixie girls.

"Calen, Lora," Art said smoothly. "This is Cinder. They are our new HR rep and significantly better than Alice."

"I would hope so," Lora said dryly. Her black eyes studied me, her pink lips drawing back to give me a forced fanged smile. "Nice to actually meet you."

"You as well, Lora," I said, offering her a smile.

She arched a brow, her eyes drifting over me.

Fuck. This was a problem. I could see how much she wanted me, and I could already feel that I wanted her.

I had to force myself not to think about that.

"Calen is my mate," Art said, looking down at him with a sly smirk.

They were definitely mates. The way their auras meshed was mesmerizing.

Calen blushed some and rose, shaking my hand. "Nice to meet you. I hope things will be better."

"Me too," I said earnestly.

I did hope they would be better.

I hoped this would be the last time I had to do something like this and that Ember and I would be able to escape. Of course, it was a pipe dream, but it was always the one I clung to when I started new missions.

Lora and I looked at each other again, our gazes locking a little longer than comfortable.

She had been flustered in the elevator, but I thought it was because she was having a bad morning. But this...

Heat rushed through me, but I forced it back.

I could not think about sex. Fuck.

"Lora— where is Mich?" Art asked, glancing around.

"Oh, he went to get breakfast for both of us," she said smoothly.

Art frowned and then shrugged. "Okay. Well, I will leave all of you to it then. Cinder, if you need help with anything, just come find me."

"Sounds good," I said, offering him a smile.

Art squeezed Calen's shoulder and then left the three of us.

Lora let out a little breath. "I'm going to go help Mich. He's been gone for a bit."

I was about to respond, but she was already moving past me and halfway across the office.

"Well," Calen said, looking after her. He chuckled and

then looked at me. "I'd get settled in before Mich gets back. He can be grumpy."

I nodded, feeling my stomach do a slow flip.

This was going to be a lot harder than I had originally thought.

# lion and the goth lamb

## MICH

My cock was hard.

I let out a long breath, trying to control my body. Trying to control everything. But it was difficult.

Something about Lora had set me off. Something about her scent. I wasn't sure what it was, but I'd had to damn near run to the room we now had so us creatures could shift if needed.

The accommodations this company had for monsters and witches in the office were good, at least. Well, mostly Inferna and Art were good at what they did. They worked well as a team, despite all the troubles initially. And Calen was good too.

I drew another breath, trying to will my body to shift back into my half form, but my muscles and bones wouldn't budge.

This wasn't good.

I always had control over my body. I had never had to

fight myself to return to a partially shifted form, even though it was uncomfortable.

This meant that...

A soft knock at the door pulled a low warning growl from me.

"Occupied," I snarled in the dark.

That scent...

I breathed it in, a moan leaving me. My cock hardened even more, and I could feel precum dripping from the tip. The spurs that lined my cock pulsed, aching to bury into something that wasn't my hand.

Fuck, surely Lora hadn't come to find me.

"Mich? Are you okay?"

Another little knock.

"Lora," I breathed.

Fuck. I closed my eyes, but it was no use. When I closed them, all I could see was her body beneath me, naked and needy. All I could imagine was her taking my entire cock over and over again, begging me to breed her.

My eyes flew open, my heart pounding.

"Mich?" she called. "Mich, what's happening?"

In all of my time, I had never had this issue. So why now? Why here at my stupid day job? If I were at my club, then at least I would be left in peace.

Why the fuck did I have this job anyway?

A little wave of frustration worked through me, and I watched as the door knob turned, twisting in the darkness.

"I'm coming in," she warned, her voice unwavering as the door cracked, and she slipped through.

Before I could stop myself, I pounced on her. The door slammed shut as I shoved her against the wall— but she didn't scream.

Her fingers dug into my fur, her nails pressing into my skin. A growl left her, surprising me.

"Hey, big guy," she whispered. "What's going on?"

"Why won't you leave me alone?" I snarled. "Why?"

I grabbed her wrists and pinned them above her head, painfully aware of her body against mine.

Her breath hitched. "I like you. I don't know what's happening, but I like you. And I was worried something was wrong."

My cock pulsed again, my knot aching. Images of Lora went through my mind again, playing like a dirty reel through my thoughts.

My scorpion tail curled around my body, the tip hovering in front of her face. Even in the veil of darkness, we could see each other perfectly. I could see the shape of her pretty face, her black eyes wide but not scared. Her silver hair was pulled back tightly, her lips parting. I could see the cute little tips of her fangs, and I realized that her wings had come out.

She had shifted some, but she wasn't scared.

"Breathe," Lora whispered.

"I can't," I murmured, my muscles relaxing slightly. "I can't. If I breathe, I smell you. And I don't know what the fuck is happening, but I feel like I want to rut you into the fucking wall, Lora."

"You were fine in the elevator," she said, her fingers gripping my fur tighter.

I let out a long moan, leaning my face in closer. Her head tipped back as I pressed my nose against her neck and breathed her in.

"Oh god," she whispered. "Mich."

Her scent changed, going from what I knew as 'normal'

Lora to something much more arousing. Her body became heated, her heartbeat speeding up.

She sounded hungry. Needy. Exactly how I wanted her to sound when she took my cock.

But not here. Not at the office where gods know who could walk in. I was close to breaking, but not close enough to let my willpower snap.

"Let me help you," she whispered.

"No," I growled. "No, Lora. We can't. We'll get caught."

"I'll make you cum, and you'll feel better. How else are you going to work?"

"No, Lora," I sneered. "Not here. Not at the office. Not when every one of our coworkers would know. I refuse to go through that."

"I don't know," Lora laughed. "I like the idea of your cum dripping from me while I work."

A moan left me as she grinned and pushed me back.

In my fully shifted form, I truly was a monster. A beast. I came from a long line of manticores, some good and some evil. I'd only ever heard of this type of thing happening if a mate was close.

Did this mean that Lora was my mate? After all this time, had my partner really just been working across from me?

I felt insane.

Lora was so small compared to me, truly reminding me of a little demonic pixie.

Mine.

"What if the witch did something to you?" Lora asked, crossing her arms.

I shook my head. The witch had done nothing but pissed me off, but I had also realized that my reaction hadn't been normal. I was cranky, but I wasn't an ass.

Not unless I was about to rut.

Which only happened to manticores if they found their mate. Or mates.

I thought about the violet-eyed witch again. Their energy had been one that would put me on my knees and happily.

Sometimes I liked to be dominant, but other times...

Other times I just really wanted to submit. I liked pleasing others. I liked being the one to take it.

It was hard to find someone that wanted to top a manticore, though.

"Mich," Lora wheezed, her eyes now on my cock.

Fuck. I bared my teeth at her and was about to growl, but she stepped closer.

"Lora," I growled. "Do not touch me like this. I could hurt you. I need to get out of here."

"How?" she snorted. "How are you going to get out of here when you clearly can't shift back right now?"

"Lora," I rasped. "I will not stop. We can't do this here. Go get Calen— he can portal me home."

"I can help," Lora said. "You forget I'm a demon too. I'm stronger than you even know."

"It's either you go get Calen, and he sends me home, or I rip off your clothes and fuck you raw, Lora. And then we explain to Inferna why we're both having to go home naked."

Lora glared for a moment and then let out a frustrated sigh, moving towards the door. She paused, turning to look back at me.

"I like the second option, Mich."

Before I could respond, she opened the door and slammed it shut.

Fuck. A groan left me, and I tried to will my body to change again with no luck.

Fucking hell, this was worse than being a horny teen. I'd been around for two hundred years, ran my own business, and worked this second job just because I could. My life was under control. I kept my personal and professional separate. Everything I did was thought out and planned.

But not this.

Not this primal reaction to Lora's scent.

My stomach gave a tug, my body shivering. She hadn't shown one bit of fear, not even in the face of a fully shifted manticore.

I would have to call my friend tonight and bail on working at the club. There was no way I'd be able to do shit like this.

Ambrosia was the monster/witch safe night club that I had started years ago with my friend Tommy, an ancient kraken shifter that liked to sling vodka and beats.

Our club did well, and we both prided ourselves on creating a space where creatures could relax some. Occasionally, a human or two would wander into our place, but due to the magical barriers we had up— they wouldn't see the monsters unless they already knew about them.

The only reason I had taken on this office job was for taxes. Because yes, even monsters paid taxes.

I drew in a breath, letting out a groan.

Plus, it wasn't like I needed much sleep. Most creatures didn't, although every now and then, I would have a month where I would pass out for a couple of days. It was enough to catch me up for most of the year.

A knock came at the door, and I frowned.

A different scent. One that was spicier. One that made me just as fucking hard.

"Go away," I rasped.

The handle turned, and I lunged as the figure slipped in. I slammed none other than the witch from the elevator against the wall.

"*You*," I snarled as the door slammed shut. "Who the fuck are you?"

Their violet eyes burned in the dark, and my own body answered my question.

*Mine.*

# *hunger*

## LORA

CALEN WAS NOWHERE TO BE FOUND, SO I WENT straight back towards the shifting room, passing by the front desk.

"Lora," I heard Anne hiss.

I paused and then went towards her, damn near launching myself over her desk. I frowned, seeing all of the scattered papers and sticky notes.

"Don't judge my desk," she said, rolling her eyes.

"I'm just surprised," I whispered, grinning. "What?"

Anne leaned in close, her diamond pupils widening. "What's going on? Why did the HR rep just go into the shifting room?"

"Wait, what?" I wheezed.

Fuck.

I looked down the hall to where the room was, looking for any signs of them.

"Cinder. They went into the shifting room," Anne

whispered quickly, her eyes wide. "Is Mich okay? Do I need to call Art or Inferna?"

"Mich is fine," I lied.

Mich would be fine if he'd just fuck me.

I'd never seen him like this.

I'd never seen anyone like this. The pure hunger burning in his gaze, the way his body wanted me. The way I wanted him. He would have devoured me, would have taken me if he wasn't so hard-headed.

"I'll go check on them, but don't let anyone else come that way," I said. "I don't know what's happening, but it's fine. Just make sure no one comes down there."

Anne nodded, arching a brow. "Alright, babe. Also, we should hang out soon."

"We should," I said quickly, smiling at her. "I'll be back."

The desk phone started to ring, and Anne winked at me, picking it up. "Warts and Claws, this is Anne. How can I help you?"

I patted the desktop and then turned, speed walking through the office, down the hall, and straight for the room.

I grabbed the doorknob and twisted it, slipping inside.

The scent of arousal hit me, making my mouth water. I let out a breath as the door shut behind me, my sight adjusting to the cool darkness.

I froze in place, my eyes widening.

Cinder was in here, and Mich had managed to shift back into his half form. Mich had Cinder's jaw firmly held in his claws, the two of them kissing like their lives depended on it.

I hadn't known what I was going to walk in on, but it certainly wasn't this.

Fuck. Watching them kiss was like a lightning rod

straight through my pussy. I bit my lower lip, my heart pounding in my chest.

Today had taken a turn, but it certainly wasn't for the worst.

Mich drew back with a low moan and then turned, his eyes meeting mine. "Lock the door," he rasped.

"What the hell is happening?" I asked.

"Lock. The. Door," Mich growled.

I reached behind me and locked it. Cinder let out a pant and started to take a step away from Mich but was immediately caught.

"Both of you," Mich whispered. "We need to go."

"Mich," Cinder rasped. "I don't know what's happening, but we need to go back to work. This will be hard to explain."

"Explain to who? You? No," Mich chuckled. "No, we need to figure this out."

"Figure what out, Mich?" I asked, feeling a little twinge of frustration.

What was happening?

"Both of you are mine," Mich said, taking a step back.

He was still naked, his cock still painfully hard. Now that I was seeing him like this, I realized that he was just as stunning. His muscles were covered in his honey-colored fur, and his cock was long and thick with a thicker knot at the base. His wings spread behind him, his horns curling back through his dark brown mane. His scorpion tail swished back and forth behind him.

Cinder stepped away now and leaned down, picking up what I realized was their jacket. They were wearing suspenders over their undershirt, their muscles no longer hiding.

Fuck. They were unbelievably sexy. Everything about them, head to toe, oozed with sensuality.

"Cinder," I whispered.

They looked up at me, the want in their violet eyes searing me.

Now, both of them looked at me like they wanted to devour me.

"I'm going into a rut," Mich said. "And that only happens to manticores when they meet their mate. Or mates, in my case. I should have known in the elevator."

Cinder's eyes widened, and they shook their head, looking back at Mich. "I can't have a mate. I can't—"

"Sorry, I don't make the rules," Mich said, shrugging. "But I know it's true. Your scent drives me insane, just like Lora's. I don't think I was as crazed for her before since you weren't here. But now that you are, we have a problem."

"I'm your HR rep," Cinder said, clearing their throat. "We can't be mates. I can't have a mate."

"Right, and you just had my tongue down your throat and your hand around my cock. HR rep or not, you're also my mate."

Cinder swallowed hard, shaking their head. "Fuck."

"Fuck is right," Mich said.

He looked at me now, waiting for me to hold his gaze. "Lora. Are you okay?"

"I... don't know what the hell is happening. But I do know we can't do anything about it here. And now that you're shifted back, we need to get back to work."

"I can't work," Mich sighed. "My cock is literally throbbing with need right now. My knot hurts. I need to fuck, or at least cum."

"I offered to help you with that," I quipped. "Or maybe Cinder can."

Cinder made a noise, shaking their head. "Fuck. This is crazy. I can't do this. It's against the rules."

"Fuck the rules," Mich chuckled. "This is just a job, Cinder."

Cinder shook their head again but then looked up at me helplessly. "You don't understand. Neither of you do. I'm sorry, but I can't do this."

"Playing hard to get. That's fine," Mich sighed, letting out a low groan. "I bet if I told you to kneel, you would."

Cinder shot him a dark look. "Funny, I think you're the one in need right now. And it will never be me on my knees, manticore."

Mich arched a brow, letting out a little chuckle. "Hmm. We can fight for dominance later when my cock is inside of you and my tongue in Lora."

"Mich," I hissed, baring my fangs.

"I will feed you first. At least I will try to be a normal date and not one that is being driven by rut brain."

"For fuck's sake," I said, letting out a helpless laugh.

"Classy," Cinder muttered.

Mich grinned, and I found myself staring at him like an idiot. This Mich was different. This Mich was not the careless manticore that I had been sitting across from for weeks now. This was not the Mich that acted like everyone was an inconvenience.

The confidence this bastard oozed was like a honey trap. He was standing in front of the two of us, completely naked and hard, like it was the most natural thing, while we were in the office.

I took a step closer to both of them, feeling the draw. I wanted this, I realized.

Fuck. I wanted to know what it would be like to be with

each of them and both of them. It had been too damn long since I'd let myself be with someone.

Cinder shook their head again. "I'm leaving. I don't care what either of you does in here. I won't report it. But I can't. Even if I wanted to, I can't."

"What does that mean?" Mich asked. "Even if you wanted to?"

Cinder was silent for a moment, and I watched a flicker of panic overcome them. They pulled their jacket on, fixing the cuffs of their sleeves.

Mich scowled, and I also found myself wondering.

Our last HR rep had been evil. There were other things going on within the company that no one but maybe Inferna, Art, and Alex was aware of. But surely Cinder was different.

I liked them too much already. Like Mich said, their scent made me want them. Everything about them made me feel like I needed them.

"I can't talk about it," Cinder said, their voice becoming firm. They straightened their shoulders, pressing their lips together. "I'm sorry. To both of you. If circumstances were different, then yes, but they aren't. I have to keep this job."

"I can probably pay you more than this job does," Mich said. "I have a club that I own. I could—"

"Do not patronize me," Cinder snapped. "I'm perfectly capable of handling myself. I've been taking care of others for years."

"Who takes care of you then?" Mich asked softly.

Cinder glared, ignoring his words. "They pay me plenty, and I like what I do. I like helping people..." their voice faltered, their violet eyes reflecting pain.

I knew what it felt like to be standing in front of people and feel alone, which was what they felt right now. I didn't like that. I didn't want them to feel that way. But I didn't know the cause, so I couldn't help.

"Fine," Mich said. "I won't chase after you, Cinder."

"I don't want you to."

I felt a little slice of pain in my chest as Cinder moved across the room, refusing to meet my gaze as they passed.

The door opened and shut quietly behind me, leaving me alone with a very hungry manticore.

Mich was silent for a moment and then arched a brow. "Am I coming off too strong?"

"Mich," I hissed, fighting off a laugh.

"I think I can control myself now, although I would like to take you home after work. If you're willing."

"I am," I said.

He crept closer, and I stilled as he came toe to toe with me. A chill worked down my spine as he loomed over me, his hand lifting. He tipped my chin up with the end of his claw, his eyes softening.

"I've liked you for a long time," he whispered. "And I want to get to know the real you."

"I want to know the real you, too," I said. "You're... different. What happened to the Mich who just wears headphones and grumbles?"

He gave me a feline smile and chuckled. "This is just a place I work, love."

My stomach did a slow flip.

He was dangerous. He had an aura about him, one that told me I would fall dangerously fast if I took the dive.

But I couldn't stop myself.

I shouldn't stop myself.

There was pain in my past. Pain from my nasty ex. Pain from the divisions within my family. Being the type of creature I was, meant that my family tree had some very dark parts to their history, and sometimes those things came up in my own life.

But why should any of that stop me? Why couldn't I have my own happiness?

"Lora," Mich murmured, running his claws through my hair.

I moaned, closing my eyes for a moment.

"Let's go back to work. And then, as soon as the day is done, come home with me. We'll figure out Cinder later. They won't be able to resist me for too long, not after a kiss like that."

I nodded, opening my eyes.

I wanted Cinder as much as I wanted Mich.

"Deal."

# fax machine fucks

## CINDER

Day one at the office had turned into both a dream and a nightmare. I spent most of the day trying to focus on my work, sifting through files, and organizing things for Alex, Inferna, and myself.

All the while, Mich ignored me like we hadn't kissed in the shifting room. Like I hadn't wanted to be with him.

Like I hadn't wanted to put him on his fucking knees.

Lora didn't ignore me, but she certainly was trying very hard not to steal long glances at me.

I felt what they felt, and it was fucking hell. I hadn't wanted this. I hadn't asked for my mates to be found.

It wasn't fair. It wasn't fair that it was these two at the office I was supposed to help destroy.

How long had it been since I had even felt something for someone? I'd been so focused on staying safe and keeping Ember out of harm's way that I had forgotten about love. What was romance when your life could crumble?

I felt my heart wrench again as I typed away on my laptop, wishing I could change things.

There had been a time when I had been able to have relationships. When I'd been able to really explore who I was and learn about my kinks, about the things that I enjoyed. I had met myself all those years ago, only for all of that to be shoved aside so I could keep my sister and me alive.

I didn't blame her. It wasn't her fault. None of this was either of our faults.

But still. I hadn't let myself even kiss anyone in what felt like ages, and kissing Mich had opened up a very needy crevice in my soul.

He acted like he was in charge. The burly manticore that liked to pretend he didn't watch everyone with a close eye. He had a double life, just like I did.

He wanted to be in charge.

He wasn't, though.

Neither would Lora.

I tried to shake the thought away, not allowing myself to truly think about what it would be like to turn these two creatures into mine.

Lora stood up from her desk, letting out a long sigh and stretching. "I need coffee, and I also need to print a few things. Cinder, do you want a cup?"

I blinked, tearing my attention away from my work.

Fuck. I wanted her. Her dark eyes were on me, her silver hair highlighted by the afternoon sun coming in from the windows.

"Uh. Sure," I said, nodding. "That sounds good."

"Okay," Lora said, winking. "Mich? Calen?"

Calen raised his head and shook it. "No, no coffee for me today."

"I'm good," Mich grumbled.

Lora nodded and then took off, leaving the three of us alone.

I watched her leave, wondering how much trouble I could actually get in if I let myself flirt with her.

Fucking hell. A lot of trouble. A LOT of trouble.

"I, uh...I'm going to go to...well, yeah," Calen said, standing up.

I scowled, trying to make sense of what he'd just said, but he was already gone.

Mich snorted. "He's been summoned."

"Oh," I said.

"Office romances are okay here, you know," Mich said. "Unless you're also evil like Alice was."

"I'm not," I hissed, looking up at him.

Was that a lie? I certainly wasn't evil like she was, but I was here to do the same work.

His honey-brown eyes met mine over the top of his computer. He arched a furry brow.

Fuck. Kissing him had been enough to make me want to do very bad things with him.

"I'm starting to wonder, though," Mich said. "You know I'm a monster. A creature, if you will."

"Yes," I said, leaning back in my seat. "And?"

"I have a great sense of smell."

"You're also going into a rut," I said. "Isn't that kind of interrupted when that happens?"

"The exact opposite," Mich growled. "I can sense even more than before. But I can smell your fear. And I don't like the idea of you being afraid of me, even if I am a monster."

"I'm not scared of creatures," I quipped. "Witches are creatures. Some of us more than others."

"Then why are you scared?"

"I don't care to share anything with you," I said, trying to keep my voice professional.

This was the hard part about being an HR rep, even when I wasn't in with the bad guys. Keeping my life away from those that talked to me.

Mich sighed and went back to his work, the silence deafening.

Fuck. Fuck, I wanted to tell him. I wanted help. I wanted a way out of all of this trouble, a way to keep my sister safe that didn't require me to deal with hell.

I was trapped.

"Cinder," Mich murmured, his gaze never leaving his computer. "If you need help, all you have to do is ask. I don't know what's going on. I don't know if you're really just this much of a workaholic or if whatever you're scared of is related to some of the things that have happened. But either way, you're not alone. And while I desperately want you in my bed naked and begging, I still recognize that there is something else happening."

I stood up, my heart pounding in my chest. "Stop," I whispered. "Stop trying. We aren't doing this. I don't want your sympathy."

"It's not sympathy," Mich said nonchalantly. "If I pretended like I wasn't attracted to you, then the problem would be that you're a shady HR agent just like Alice. The problem would be that there are things none of us employees know about in regards to the company merger that has to do with all of us, but we are kept in the dark. Believe me, I'm the first one to know that our world isn't pretty."

"Well, then why are you pressing so hard?" I snapped. "Why are you trying to corner me into telling you what's happening?"

Mich's gaze snapped up, and I cursed under my breath.

"Don't speak to me," I muttered, snatching up my laptop.

I grabbed my stack of papers and tucked it under my arm, leaving the nosy but sexy manticore before I said too much more.

Fuck. If someone had heard that…if someone had heard that, and it got back to the wrong ears, then I was fucked.

That's how closely they watched this office.

I held back the tears, shoving down my emotions as I moved across the floor. I could feel the eyes of monsters and witches alike following me as I headed down the hall, away from the main work area.

The way this office was set up was almost like a maze. There was the main floor, which was where everyone worked. There was the front desk, and then through a doorway, there was an elevator.

But there was also a hall that led to the shifting room. Then there were some other empty offices that I wanted to hide in, away from prying eyes.

Away from Mich and Lora.

If I let them get close, then they would be in danger. If I let them get to know me, if I let them discover the truth—then everything would be jeopardized.

I rounded the corner and then gasped as Lora ran straight into me.

"Fuck," she squealed.

The coffee she was holding spilled forward, splashing all over me. My laptop hit the floor, the papers flying everywhere.

"Oh fuck," Lora gasped. "Oh my god, are you okay? That's hot!"

Fuck. I felt the burn now and promptly stepped into the

room to our left. Lora immediately closed the door behind us, rushing to me.

The searing pain made me hiss, and I yanked off my jacket. Lora was already on me, her little talons ripping the front of my shirt open and tearing the burning fabric away from my skin.

"Oh, Cinder," she gasped, her voice panicked. "I'm so sorry. I can get you ice—"

"It's okay," I groaned, leaning against the fax machine.

We'd stepped into the printer and supply room, the smell of ink and warm paper surrounding us.

My skin was still burning as if it'd soaked up the coffee. My endorphins had kicked in, numbing me enough to where I could speak.

"It's not that bad." I winced, looking down.

Fuck, I was already blistering around the edge of the dark red splotch.

"Okay, okay," Lora said quickly. "Listen, I'm a demon, but I'm also fae. I'm a pixie, and my saliva has healing properties."

"What does that have to do with being a fae demon?" I asked, confused.

"Just let me lick you," Lora said. "It'll make the pain go away."

We stared at each other for a moment. My shirt was ripped open, and her hands were gripping my suspenders, my body pressed against the fax machine. Her black eyes were wide, her words honest.

Just let me lick you.

"Do I have your consent?" Lora whispered.

Fuck.

Under other circumstances, having her lick me would be a dream come true. But this...

Fuck it. The numbness started to wear off, the pain growing stronger. There was something to be said about how fucking painful coffee burns could be.

"Yes," I said, my voice hoarse. My sex pulsed, my body aching for her touch.

Lora nodded, and I caught that wicked glint. The one that made my entire body feel like it was being bathed in sultry flames.

"Cinder," she whispered. "I promise I won't bite."

I wanted her to, though. I wanted to know what her little fangs would feel like at my neck.

She leaned down and parted her lips, the tip of her tongue tracing the edge of the burn. I gasped, my head falling back as she began to lick me carefully and methodically.

She was right. The pain began to subside, and I found myself moaning, my sex throbbing. I wanted to be with her, to fuck her.

I looked down, watching her intently now. Her silver bangs were swept to the side from where she had run her hands through her hair, her fangs glinting in the yellow office lighting as she licked me.

I wanted her to lick me all over.

"Lora," I whispered, every sane thought going out the window.

She looked up at me, her eyes locking with mine as she lapped at my skin. The coffee had spilled right on my abs, and she took her time tracing the indentations of the muscles.

She paused for a moment, licking her lips. Her pale skin had turned rosy, her aura the color of lust.

"Cinder," she murmured. "Did that help?"

"Yes," I whispered hoarsely. "In more ways than one. I

need you."

I had a thousand reasons not to do this but only needed one to make me toss out all of my worries— even if it was just for a moment.

"I need you too," she said. "I want you. I want whatever this is."

I leaned down, tipping her chin up. I pressed my forehead to hers, breathing in her scent. I knew she was taking in mine, reading me like an open book.

I wished she could breathe in my secrets so I didn't have to feel scared anymore. I wish I didn't have to take on the things I did alone.

Her hand slid up my chest, all the way up to cup my jaw. Her palm was warm against my skin. I felt my magic bubbling up to the surface, reaching for her like a flower reaching for the sun.

Finally, our lips met. She melted against me, a soft little moan leaving her. It was the kind of sound that would undo someone, the kind of noise that would linger in my memories forever.

Her lips parted, and our tongues met, the two of us growing more demanding with each second that passed. My hands slid down to her waist, and I found myself lifting her and turning, setting her on the fax machine.

A little growl of surprise left her as we devoured each other, lust egging us on.

She broke the kiss with a gasp, her fingers moving up to the buttons of her blouse. She undid them quickly, and I leaned forward, kissing down her neck, across her chest, and down between her breasts.

"Fuck," I groaned. "You're perfect."

"So are you," she gasped.

My sex throbbed again, and I moaned, pushing her

blouse down off her shoulders. She was wearing a sheer black bra with a demon summoning charm at the center.

I was about to reach around and unhook it when a knock came at the door, startling both of us.

Our faces dropped, and I pulled away, cursing under my breath.

"Hello?"

Fuck, it was Inferna.

"Hey. I need copy paper. Also, there's coffee and a laptop, and papers everywhere in the hall. Is everything okay? Hello? I can hear you breathing."

"Hold on!" Lora called, buttoning her shirt back up.

She hopped off the fax machine and grabbed me, shoving me back against it. She gave me a stern 'stay put' expression and turned, composing herself before going to the door.

She opened it just as the doorknob started to rattle, revealing Inferna.

"Lora," Inferna said, scowling. She peeked around and arched a brow, her lips twisting devilishly.

"It's not what you think," I said quickly.

"I spilled coffee on Cinder, and it burned them, so I used some magic to heal them," Lora said quickly.

"Oh?" Inferna said as if she weren't a succubus who fed off sexual tension like it was a fucking buffet. Her dark eyes fell down to my torn shirt. "Ah. Okay, then. Well, there is a first aid kit at Anne's desk. And it has some special creams and stuff that would keep you from having to lick Cinder's abs, Lora."

Lora and I both blanched as Inferna slipped by her, grabbed a pack of copy paper, and then darted back out. She paused, her heart-shaped tail swishing behind her.

"Welcome to Warts & Claws, Cinder. I think you'll do just fine."

Before either one of us could say anything, she let out a little cackle and left us stunned.

"Oh, for fuck's sake," Lora whispered.

"Fuck. Fuck, I should go talk to her," I said, panic creeping in.

She turned, giving me a hard look. "Go talk to her, and then once work is over, you're coming home with Mich and me. We're going to figure out whatever the fuck this is. Understood?"

"Yes," I whispered, helpless now.

I'd already fucked up and couldn't find the willpower to stop myself from doing it again.

# *master*

## MICH

As soon as the clock hit 6 p.m., the three of us were up and out of our seats in the blink of an eye.

I wasn't sure what happened, but after Cinder and Lora had come back earlier— Cinder informed me they would be joining me after work.

I'd felt a little sense of victory then, but now I was nervous.

This was different. This wasn't like I was taking home some random monster or witch for the night. These were two coworkers, two people I had met in the office.

Still...

The three of us stepped into the elevator, silence settling over us as it took us down to the first floor. The doors slid open, and I waited for the two of them to walk ahead, only for them to follow me.

I would drive Lora while Cinder would be taking their car. They'd insisted on taking a different direction, which was a reminder that there was something going on— but I had a hard time caring.

I had a hard time worrying when all I could think about was how much I needed to mate. I needed to fuck. My cock had been aching for both of them, precum threatening to drip from the tip.

I'd been so patient all day long. All fucking day.

"I will meet you both there," Cinder said quickly as we hit the parking garage.

I nodded, Lora trailing after me. "Call if you get lost."

Cinder nodded, and I watched them cross over to their car.

They were nervous.

Lora let out a little breath. "I want them, but I'm worried for them."

"Me too," I said, frowning.

Maybe it was because they were meant to be mine, but I felt a connection to Cinder. And that connection told me they were in danger.

Maybe they would eventually trust Lora and me enough to tell us.

"Do you want me to drive?" Lora asked.

"We could fly," I said, smiling a little. "Might help the tension some. I don't care about flying back in the morning."

"Alright," Lora agreed, giving me a cute fanged grin.

I was eager to see her wings. She took a step back, and I watched as they appeared. They reminded me of stained glass, but I knew they were stronger than steel. They were smaller than mine but the perfect size to carry her.

Monsters and witches moved around us, along with humans that also worked in the building. The humans didn't see us as us, though, blind to what we really looked like. It made things fun sometimes, especially when a human naturally gave me space without realizing why.

"Alright," I said. "Last one there has to strip first."

My wings pushed off, and Lora laughed, calling me a jackass as her own wings took her up into the air. We made our way to the exit of the garage and flew straight up, flying up the side of the building.

The sunset glared off the glass, the reflections of our beautiful but monstrous forms shining as we cleared the building.

The air had my favorite type of crispness. The kind that made me want to fly forever. The sky was a wash of pink and peach, scarred by the golden streak of the sun. I glanced behind me to catch a glimpse of Lora basking in the warm glow.

Within a few minutes, the two of us landed on the balcony of my apartment. I turned in time to keep her from stumbling and then lifted her up, needing her.

Fuck, I needed her so badly.

Her arms immediately wound around my neck, and she pulled me into a heated kiss, her legs wrapping around my waist. She still had a hint of Cinder's taste, and I wanted to fucking devour her.

I reached behind me and slid open the balcony door, taking her inside. She moaned against me, never letting go.

I slid the balcony door closed and then carried her to my couch, lowering her down to the cushion. My knees hit the floor, and I found myself parting her legs, my cock desperate.

I felt like I had been bathed in fire. The need to mate her was so strong, to rut into her sweet body and feel her cum around me.

But something was missing...

The doorbell rang, and I drew back, my clouded thoughts clearing for a moment. Lora started to get up, but I pushed her back down, giving a little growl.

"Sit," I commanded, rising.

I went to the door, pulling it open quickly and yanking in my other mate.

I wasn't patient anymore, and I didn't want to be. Cinder let out a yelp as I shoved them against the door, giving them the same heated kiss I'd had with Lora.

Cinder didn't push back this time, instead pressing their body to mine. I could feel the hardness of their sex against mine, straining to be touched.

Cinder gasped, pulling back. Their violet and black eyes shimmered, their lips pulling back into a helpless smile. "Hey."

"Hi," I breathed.

They looked past me to Lora, their eyes widening and a gasp leaving them.

I turned and damn near fell to my knees.

Lora had stripped off her clothes, all except for the black lingerie that strapped her body. She was seated on my couch now, her legs spread and her silver hair untied.

Fuck.

"Lora," Cinder whispered. "Fuck."

"Fuck indeed," I growled. "Fuck."

We both stared at her like idiots, and she smiled, her black eyes twinkling with delight. Her wings were still out, adding to her delicate monster appearance.

"Before we do this, we should talk about what we like and dislike," Cinder said, their voice wavering for a moment. "Fuck, Lora," they sighed. "I can't even think straight between the two of you."

Lora giggled. "Well, how about both of you come and sit then? Instead of gawking."

"Easier said than done," I mumbled, looking down at my cock.

My pants were ready to fucking split.

But Cinder was right. We needed to discuss these things.

I had tastes. Preferences. Things that I enjoyed. And under normal circumstances, I would actually discuss them in depth and make sure the person I was with was someone I had chemistry with. Someone I could talk frankly with.

Instead, all I could think about was that I was desperate to cum. I was desperate to mate both Cinder and Lora over and over again until the three of us were gloriously satisfied.

Cinder let out a breath and then went to the sofa, taking a seat next to Lora. They propped their arm up on the back of the couch, looking over at me.

"Come on, big guy," Lora teased me.

I let out a little growl but listened, going to her and taking her opposite side.

"You first," Lora said, poking my bicep. "Since you're the one in a rut."

"Normally, I would be much better about this," I said, letting out a helpless moan as heat crashed into my veins. My senses were starting to go crazy, the fever of need setting in. "I like..."

I paused for a moment, trying to center myself.

This entire time with the two of them, I had been behaving more dominant. But that wasn't what I wanted in the bedroom.

"May I speak?" Cinder asked, leaning forward a little.

I nodded, my stomach twisting.

"I don't want to put words in your mouth, but you're in

a rut. A heat, if you will. And now that I've come to terms with the fact that I am doing this, I'm not going to act any different than who I am. You're a manticore, Mich. I imagine that everyone in the world thinks you should dominate this little pixie and witch, right? But that's not what you want."

I stared at them, feeling as if I had just taken off my mask and shown who I truly was.

What they said was right.

The way they said it also told me I had been wrong about them.

Between the three of us, Cinder would be the most dominant.

"Correct," I whispered.

Cinder nodded and then looked at Lora. "And you?"

Lora stared at them for a moment, her cheeks turning pink. "I like to submit," she whispered. "But it takes a lot of trust. I'm kinky, I won't hide that."

"I think all three of us are," I said, swallowing hard.

Lora nodded, holding her breath for a moment. "I just... It's been a long time. And it takes trust to truly allow myself to go to that place."

The subspace. The only place I could truly forget everything but the person in front of me. I craved to be there, but it took some work. It also took a lot of trust and finding someone willing to put a manticore on his knees was hard.

Cinder gave a patient smile. "I think the difficulty here, at least between the two of you, is that you know each other in a work environment. You've only known me since this morning, and... when I'm at work, I have to be careful. It's different."

"It is," Lora said.

"So, what if we pretend that we don't work together? And what if we allow ourselves to finally have a little fun? It's been too long for me, and I... I want this. I haven't been with anyone in a very long time," Cinder said. "I like being in control. And I like the idea of letting myself do that."

"I like the idea of you doing that," I mumbled, looking away.

"Are you ashamed?" Cinder asked bluntly.

"No," I said, looking back at them. "No. I just struggle with letting myself go sometimes."

"Same," Lora whispered.

Cinder nodded, eyes softening. "Me as well."

I took a deep breath, my shoulders finally relaxing. I still felt like I was on fire, my cock was still painfully hard, but I was able to breathe now without feeling like I was going to explode.

"I can tell you what I want," Cinder said. "And you can both tell me yes or no."

Lora and I both leaned closer.

Cinder smirked a little, their voice becoming soft and seductive. I felt like I was being lured in by a siren, everything about them enchanting me.

"I want to be a Master. I want to have a pet. Someone that will do the things I want them to do. Someone that likes to serve. I want someone that will be a footstool if I ask them to. I want someone that will only orgasm when I allow them to. I want someone that will obey me. And in return, I want to care for them. I want to love them. I want to be able to have a happy life where I can appreciate the way they care for me because servicing me brings them happiness. I want someone who will want the things I ask of them. Those are the things I want. I'm not your typical Dom or Master or

Mistress. I'm not your typical alpha person. But I try to be authentic to myself, and I know these are the things I want."

I felt like my world had been turned upside down.

I wanted to please Cinder.

Fuck. It was so hard to allow myself that, but it was true.

"Well," Lora whispered. "A lot of those things take time."

"They do," Cinder agreed. "You are correct. We can start with play, though, if both of you are willing."

"I'm willing," I said.

"I am too," Lora whispered.

"What about your safe words? Or any limits I should know about?" Cinder asked.

"Mine is *summon*," Lora answered. "And I don't like being blindfolded or tied up. Everything else is fine. I like pain. I like electricity. I like knife play too...."

Cinder nodded, turning their gaze onto me.

"*Red* is my safeword," I answered, clearing my throat. "I...I will be your footstool if you want."

Cinder chuckled. "Go on, Mich."

"Limits— I don't like food play. I can't think of anything else right now that is a limit."

"Excellent. Well, I have two limits," Cinder said, surprising me. "I prefer my genitalia to be referred to as my 'sex'. So if you are begging me, you are begging to take my sex. You are begging me to fuck you, mate you, breed you, but all with my sex. Second, we still have to at least pretend to be professional in the office."

"We can try our best," I said.

Lora nodded, sweeping her silver hair back. "We can try, Cinder. Is your burn from earlier okay?"

"It's good," Cinder said, arching a black brow. "I think I'm going to use that ability to my advantage."

Fuck. I wanted to know what they meant by that.

Cinder's eyes flashed, and they leaned back. The air around them shifted, and I felt my cock throb.

"Good then. Well, from this moment until our scene is done, you may call me Master. And your Master needs somewhere to hang their clothes."

# *service*

## LORA

CINDER BENT ME OVER THE COUCH, THEIR FINGERS grazing over the straps of my panties. They tugged on one, letting it snap back against my skin.

"Stay," they commanded.

"Yes, Master," I whispered.

Cinder's fingertips grazed over my skin, little sparks making me gasp. My wings fluttered for a moment, reflecting the same little tremors that worked through my pussy.

My heart beat rapidly in my chest, and I felt my blood surging through my veins. I was so fucking wet already, desperate to be touched.

I wanted to lick them again. I wanted to taste their body, to look up at them like they were the center of the universe.

"*Pet*," Cinder whispered, "stay exactly like this. Understand?"

"Yes, Master."

Cinder stepped away, and I wanted to follow them with my eyes, but I resisted. I obeyed them.

"Slave," Cinder said. "I need a seat right here behind Lora."

I bit my lower lip, wanting to look between my legs. I couldn't, though. I closed my eyes instead as Mich moved, shuffling behind me. He let out a little groan, and I knew he had gotten on all fours behind me.

"Good. Seats don't speak, and neither do hangers that hold clothing. They are objects. Understood?"

I nodded silently, my mind spiraling.

I wanted this. I wanted to do exactly as they wanted, and I wanted to do my very best at it.

I heard the sound of Cinder's jacket sliding off their body, and then they draped it over my back. My pussy throbbed as I was ignored, fighting not to whimper or make any noises. Fighting to be still.

I could hear Mich's breaths, could scent his arousal. How fucking hard he was for me, for our Master.

Cinder undid their suspenders and then began to unbutton their dress shirt. They draped their clothing over me, going until I imagined that they were completely undressed.

They reached down and wrapped their hand in my hair, pushing my head down so that I could see between my legs. I could see Mich now, could see how he waited. Waited just like I did.

"I think I need to inspect this hanger," Cinder said as they moved behind me.

Mich's breath hitched, and he fought a moan as Cinder sat on his back. Cinder was still wearing underwear, a black lace thong that made my entire body ache.

Fuck, they were so hot. The fact that they had been wearing that all day underneath an unassuming suit...

Cinder lifted their hand, their fingertips tracing my pussy. I was unable to stop the noise that left me.

They let out a little hiss, pinching my ass cheek. The pain was sharp and sudden, there and then gone within a moment.

I choked on a squeal, fighting for silence. It was a challenge, but god damn it. God damn it, I wanted to do it well.

Cinder pulled my underwear to the side, rubbing their thumb over my clit.

Oh fuck.

This was going to be impossible.

"Mm, such a pretty clit," Cinder murmured. "You should see her clit, slave. I bet you'd like to, wouldn't you? You may speak."

"Yes," Mich groaned. "Fuck. Cinder, please."

The sound of Cinder smacking Mich's ass echoed through the apartment.

"Master," Mich moaned, correcting himself.

"There we go," Cinder chuckled. "Not yet. If my little pet can be a good clothes hanger for another three minutes, then I will let her cum. And then I will let you taste her. Let you fuck her."

Cinder spread my pussy wide with one hand, dipping two fingers inside of me for just a moment.

FUCK. It took every ounce of control not to cry out. I was so fucking wet, so needy.

Their thumb began to move my clit in gentle circles, lazily as if they weren't driving me absolutely insane. My knees weakened as they pushed their fingers inside of me again, starting a rhythm that made me pant.

Tears filled my eyes as I fought myself. I was waging war against all of the sounds I wanted to make, begging my body not to betray me. I wanted to be good. I wanted to please them.

I *had to* please them.

I'd needed this for so long. It felt like it had been eons since I had been taken like this— and it had been even longer since I'd allowed myself to truly submit.

My mind began to swim, my thoughts fading as I allowed myself to simply be. I was to be their clothes hanger, that was it. To serve them how they wanted.

Pleasure began to build up, winding up inside of me. Threatening to drag me down into a storm of cries.

"Not too much longer," Cinder murmured, still playing with me. Torturing me. "Such a good little pet. I like seeing you like this, especially after you cleaned me up earlier. You drove me crazy with that demon tongue of yours."

I held onto my words, biting back a groan. Sweat dripped down my forehead, my wings fighting not to twitch.

"One more minute," Cinder said.

Only one more—

I swallowed a squeal as Cinder plunged two of their fingers inside of me, thrusting them in further as their thumb continued to rub my clit. My entire body tensed, my heart pounding in my chest.

FUCK. Pleasure ran through me, stabbing me like a hot iron. Tears filled my eyes as I tried not to think about how close I was to cumming. I tried not to think about the way they were making me feel.

"Such a naughty little pet," Cinder chuckled. "So wet. Are you ready to take Mich's cock? I'm sure he would like that."

I was. I wanted Mich just as much as I wanted Cinder,

and his scent was driving me crazy. I could taste his arousal, every breath a reminder of how fucking badly he needed to mate.

"I can feel him shaking beneath me," Cinder said. "And it's not because I'm sitting on him. It's because he's so fucking desperate to fill this tight pussy with his cock. He's been waiting all day. I wonder how it felt earlier when he realized he was going into a rut...."

Blood welled from where my teeth bit into my bottom lip, the pain tearing my focus away from the waves of ecstasy pumping through me.

Cinder pulled their hand free and shoved me down onto the couch, gripping my hair. "Speak," they whispered.

"FUCK!" I gasped, letting out a long moan.

Cinder gave me a wicked smile and let me go, leaving me in a puddle of gasps and moans.

"Slave," Cinder said, leaning down.

I looked behind me, panting as Cinder cupped Mich's head and kissed him. They drew back and then straightened.

"Open your mouth," Cinder commanded.

Mich immediately obeyed, his fangs flashing in the lighting of his apartment.

Cinder offered him the two fingers that had been inside of me, and Mich sucked them, his honey eyes burning with adoration and need.

His wings spread behind him, his scorpion tail curling around. He let out a soft growl, his head tipping back.

"Strip," Cinder commanded him.

Mich immediately pulled off his shirt and pants, followed by his underwear. My eyes immediately fell down to his cock as it sprang free, a gasp leaving me.

His cock was crimson red and about ten inches long, thick,

and covered in small spurs along the ridge. There was even a knot at the base, one meant to keep all of his cum inside of me.

I stared, my cheeks turning bright red.

"So small," Cinder sighed.

I choked, drawing Cinder's violet gaze.

"Oh?" Cinder asked. "You can't handle a cock like this, pet?"

"I can," I whispered.

My pussy throbbed, still wet from everything they had done to me.

Cinder arched a dark brow, looking back down at Mich.

"Master," Mich whispered. "Please allow me to touch her. To fuck her."

Cinder ran their fingers through Mich's mane, tugging on the hair for a moment. They tsked, their smile softening. "Okay, little slave. Fuck her."

Mich didn't hesitate, and neither did I. I turned to meet him, immediately winding my arms around his head. He lifted me, bringing my legs around his waist.

Cinder took a seat on the couch, leaning back and watching us with a devilish smile. "Go on," they urged. "I want to watch. I want to see if she can really take it."

"I can," I rasped. "I can. I'll take it if you tell me to."

Cinder's eyes darkened, and they nodded, watching the two of us intently.

Mich turned, using his tail to swipe everything off the coffee table in the center of the living room. Things crashed to the floor, and I was immediately laid down, the tip of his cock rubbing against my entrance.

"Mich," I moaned. "Fuck. Please. I need this!"

I was so desperate to be filled. I had never taken a cock

as big as his, nor one with spurs, but I was a little monster, too, after all.

Mich leaned down, dragging his rough tongue all the way down my body. I gasped, my nipples hardening as he licked me. He took one of them between his teeth, giving me a bite.

I arched against the table, a moan leaving me as the pain flared. Mich groaned, sucking me. Toying with me.

"I'm going to breed you for our Master," Mich rasped. "To prove I am a good servant."

"Yes," I groaned. "Please. I need you inside of me."

Mich's claws dug into the tabletop next to my head, and he groaned. He moved forward, rubbing my entrance with the head of his cock.

"If it hurts, tell me," he rasped. "But fuck. I have to fuck you, Lora. I need you."

"Tell him," Cinder said. "Tell him how much you've wanted his cock in your little monster cunt."

Cinder's words made my entire body burn, the ache to be fucked until I couldn't walk straight returning with a vengeance.

"Please, Mich," I whispered. I reached up and grabbed his face, holding his gaze. "I've wanted you for so long. I want to be with you, to be fucked by you. I can't wait to feel you inside of me."

Mich shivered and reached down between us, spreading me wide as he began to move forward. My eyes fluttered, my head falling back.

The first inch was already enough to make me cry out, followed by the second and third. The first spur rubbed against me as it was pushed inside, stroking the sensitive spot on my upper wall.

"Oh fuck," I growled, biting my lip again. Pain flashed through me, making my nipples harden.

I heard Cinder's moan and arched my head back, opening my eyes. I met their gaze and felt pure euphoria flush through me.

They were watching the two of us, pulling their sex free of the lace thong. They began stroking themself, watching us as Mich dragged his cock back and then shoved it back in.

A scream left me, but my gaze didn't break from theirs.

"Harder," I moaned, tears blurring my vision.

Mich grunted and then thrust more, giving me every inch this time. The sound of our skin slapping together echoed through the apartment as he began to fuck me, moving into a brutal rhythm.

The coffee table groaned beneath us, and I cried out as I took every fucking spur and every inch of Mich. He stopped holding back and started rutting into me, losing himself to the haze of need that had been torturing him since this morning.

Cinder watched still, their moans of pleasure edging me.

My first orgasm hit, and I didn't hold back, allowing myself to scream. A flood of heat washed over me, my body quaking.

"Yes," Cinder purred. "Good girl. Look at how good she is for you, Mich."

I groaned, my head spinning.

Mich growled, his claws raking down my sides. I cried out, but the pain was almost just as hot as the feeling of his cock thrusting in and out of me. He gripped my waist, pinning me in place as he pumped into me.

"Breed my pet, slave," Cinder commanded.

"Fuck," Mich groaned. "I'm so close."

I heard Cinder stand up, and they came over to us, standing at the edge of the table. I stared up at them as they stroked themself and opened my mouth, wanting to take whatever they would give me.

"Are you going to cum with me, slave?" Cinder taunted.

"Yes," Mich gasped.

"Three," Cinder said, their voice becoming seductive.

I felt like I was under their spell, completely enchanted by them.

"Two," Cinder growled.

Mich shuddered, so close now. Just barely hanging on.

"One. Now," Cinder commanded.

I gasped as Mich gave one final thrust, shoving his knot inside of me. He let out a long moan, finally cumming. His heat spilled inside of me the same moment Cinder came on my breasts.

Fuck. This was glorious. I looked between the two of them, enjoying their expressions. My own body was relaxed but still buzzing from my own orgasm, Mich still pumping his cum inside of me. His knot spread me wide, keeping every drop inside.

After a few moments, Mich lowered his head, licking up the drops of Cinder's cum as he panted. He gave another little thrust, and I moaned as pleasure burst through me again.

Cinder chuckled at the reaction, leaning down to kiss me. I arched my head back, opening my mouth so their tongue could brush against mine.

They pulled back with a gentle smile. "That was fun."

"That was fun," I rasped, letting out a little giggle.

Mich let out a moan, resting his head on my chest. His cock was still buried inside of me, his knot pulsing.

"I have a large shower," Mich mumbled. "I think we should use it. And then maybe some dinner."

"That sounds good," Cinder said. "I could go for some Chinese food."

"We could watch that show about the office, too," I said, grinning.

I liked watching a sitcom about humans in the office. Every time I had a bad day, it made me laugh.

Mich snorted, lifting his head. He planted a kiss on me and nuzzled me again. "Sure. We can do all of those things. Once my knot goes down."

"And then get some rest for tomorrow," Cinder said.

I nodded, smiling to myself.

It was only Monday, but it seemed like the rest of this week was going to be interesting.

# one on one

## CINDER

It was only 10 a.m., but I was already beyond annoyed.

I sat across from Inferna and Alex, the three of us watching the giant screen as the board of directors droned on about changes. Alex had already made it clear that the changes he was implementing here first would need to be implemented in the other offices around the country.

The amazing thing was, everyone acted like everything was fine.

Meanwhile, all I could really find myself caring about was what had happened last night.

I turned my head slightly, glancing at the clock. It had only been an hour, but I already ached to be next to Mich or Lora. Both of them, really.

Last night had been the first time since I could remember that I had allowed myself to really let go. The things I enjoyed in the bedroom were things the two of them seemed to enjoy as well. Edging Lora until she could barely breathe and then watching Mich fuck her had been the hottest thing I'd ever seen, and I wanted to do it again.

In fact, I was supposed to be paying attention to this fucking meeting, but all I could think about was what I wanted to try next.

The call lasted another ten minutes and then finally ended. Inferna cleared her throat, and Alex sighed, shaking his head.

"Fucking hell— you know what would be nice? If people just listened to me," Alex grumbled. "As if I'm not the one that makes the decisions. Fucking witchy bitches."

"Alex," Inferna scolded, biting back a laugh.

Alex threw up his hands, giving me a wicked grin. "Sorry. You can report me to HR."

I snorted, unable to hide my smile. "I think bad language is the least of our worries right now."

"Indeed," Alex agreed, leaning back in his chair. "Today, you will start meeting with employees one on one. And then later this week, we will have the new hires starting. The ones that escaped Alice and Claude."

"Is there a reason for the one on ones?" I asked. "I'm just not sure what I'm bringing."

"Just general check-ins. All the performance evaluation stuff is off the table right now, given all the things that have happened. But, we still need to just check in," Inferna said, giving me a hard look.

She fucking knew what she had seen yesterday, and she was amused by it. That unnerved me.

"I think you could start with Lora," Inferna said. "In fact, why don't you start with your table? My Calen, and then your Lora and Mich. Oh, I mean just Lora and Mich."

It took every ounce of control not to let my expression waver.

Fucking succubus. Of course, she would be able to smell sex on the three of us.

I gave her a small smile. "I guess I can do that."

Alex clapped his hands, making me jump as he stood up. "Excellent. Good work. I'm going to go talk to Anne and see if she can help me with some stuff."

Inferna arched a brow, watching our boss leave the two of us. I watched him walk out the door, waving his hand and dismissing the meeting.

He was....he was a conundrum.

"Well then," Inferna said. "So, how are you feeling about everything?"

"Good," I said, meeting her gaze.

She was picking me over like a shark and enjoying every moment of it. I could see why she was the boss.

"Mhm. Is your stomach okay?"

"My stomach?" I asked.

Inferna blinked, waiting for me to realize what she meant, and then it dawned on me.

The coffee. The spill. Lora's tongue on me.

Fuck.

I couldn't think about Lora's tongue on me.

"Oh! Yeah, it's fine. I'm a creature, after all," I said. "I heal pretty fast."

Inferna nodded, her fangs glinting as she gave me a wicked grin. "Well. You should know one thing about me, Cinder."

"And what is that?" I asked.

Inferna cocked her head, her demeanor becoming even more fierce. "I will eat you alive if you harm Lora or Mich."

"I don't know what you're talking about," I lied.

Inferna waved her hand at me, snorting. "Don't. I can see what's happening. I don't have anything against it. But, I am concerned about the fact that you are an HR rep. And that there are still bad things going on."

It was on the tip of my tongue suddenly. The urge to tell her about everything. To tell her about the ones that were bad.

Three of those faces on the committee had just been pleasant masks of true monsters. Acting as if they belonged in this world of apps and computers. Pretending they weren't trying to do very evil things.

"Cinder," Inferna said, lowering her voice. "I'm trying to tell you that I am a friend. You know that, right? You know I wouldn't let anything happen to you either."

"You can't promise anything," I whispered, the words coming out before I could stop them.

A surge of panic worked through me, a stark reminder that my sister was in danger when I acted like this. Inferna could not protect us. No one could.

Fuck. What the fuck was I even doing with Mich or Lora? Yesterday had been a moment of weakness, but it had to stop.

Pain ripped through my heart at the thought of shutting down those connections.

Inferna stood up, looking down at me. Her horns shone in the morning light, her blazer and pants perfectly pressed. "When you need me, I will be here. I won't force you to tell me, but I want you to know that you're not alone. Regardless of what you think or whatever you have been told. I have stronger connections than any of these bastards, and they are being watched now by the fucking devil himself. Literally. Lucifer is one of my uncles."

Somehow that didn't surprise me.

"I hear you," I whispered.

Inferna nodded and then cleared her throat, picking up her laptop and papers. "I will be in my office if you need me. Have fun on those one on ones."

With that, she left me alone, the sound of her heels clicking on the tiles as she walked away.

I let out a sigh, looking up at the window and the building across the street.

He was always watching us. Always. They would watch when I left, when I arrived.

That's why I had insisted on driving myself to Mich's apartment. I had done everything I could to make sure I wasn't being tracked.

It had worked. But how long would it take before one of them found out?

Not to mention, there were secret agents. There were sleepers that worked in this office that not even I knew about.

I had to be careful.

I stood up, grabbed all my stuff, and headed out of the office to the elevator. Why Alex had a whole floor to himself was beyond me, but I would be using one of the offices up here to do the one on ones since it was quiet.

I hated that. I didn't want anyone to think they were in trouble. But maybe I could win over more people in the office.

The elevator doors slid open, and my eyes widened. None other than Mich was standing there.

"Hey," he said, giving me a sheepish smile. "Art sent me up. Said it was for the one-on-one."

"Oh," I said, taking a step back so Mich could come in.

His aura was saturated again, dripping with need. With lust.

Fuck.

"Mich," I whispered, my voice going hoarse. "Did your rut not break last night?"

"No," he said, his eyes softening. "No. I'm dying right now, but it is what it is. I went ahead and called in at the club for the rest of the week and let my friend know."

"Club?" I asked.

"Oh," Mich said. "I own a club with my friend Tommy. That's my actual job, this one is just to help with taxes. Plus, I like money. And my apartment."

"Oh," I said. "What's the club called?"

"Ambrosia," he said, smiling despite the fact that his cock was getting harder in his pants. "It's a creature club."

I stared at him for a moment, trying to apply this business casual manticore to one that would own a club for monsters. There were moments when he stopped masking, though, ones where he exuded confidence and charm.

"We should go sometime," I said without thinking.

Fuck. What was I doing?

"This weekend, I'll take you and Lora out," he said.

I wanted to help him. Fuck.

Fuck. Why did I even care about him?!

"Come with me," I growled, turning and heading back into the main office.

I went to a room that was the furthest away from everything, opening the door for the two of us. Mich slipped inside, and I slammed it shut.

The lights were off, the blinds pulled down.

Mich turned to look at me, and my eyes fell down to his cock.

He was wearing khaki pants today, and it didn't do much to hide everything down there.

"Really?" I growled.

"Master," Mich whispered, a hungry plea.

Fucking hell. I damn near tossed my things onto one of the chairs and then went to him, shoving him back onto the desk. Pens went flying, the supplies hitting the floor as I spread him back.

"Pants off," I commanded.

Mich nodded, immediately unbuttoning them and then kicking them off.

His cock sprang free, and he let out a helpless moan.

"Such a helpless little bitch," I muttered. "I'm trying to work. To fucking do my job. And here you are, hard and needy."

"Yes, Master," Mich moaned. "I can't help it. I can't stop myself."

"Yeah, because you're a little needy bitch," I snapped.

With the flick of my hand, I used my magic to lock and block the door. The room buzzed with the tint of the spell, the words tumbling from my lips.

Now I would know if someone came up to the door.

"One on one," I growled. "Your one-on-one will be you cumming so that you can behave the rest of the day."

"Yes, Master," he gasped. "Please."

"I'm going to suck your cock, and while I'm doing that, I want you to tell me about your day so far. Every detail. Starting with when I left this morning."

Mich groaned, his massive wings draping over the sides of the desk I had him spread on. His body was hot, his cock throbbing with need.

I reached up and unbuttoned his shirt, letting out a satisfied hum as I ran my hands down his chest.

"Master," Mich gasped. "Shit. I can't even remember my day."

I took hold of his cock and began stroking it, pausing to

run my fingertips over the spurs. I paused, gripping his knot and squeezing.

His entire body reacted, a long groan leaving him.

The fact that Lora had taken every inch was amazing, especially with the spurs.

I parted my lips and spat, letting it hit the tip of his cock. I started to work it up and down his shaft, stroking him a little harder.

"Fuck."

"Start talking," I commanded. "We don't have much time, slave. If you don't cum by the time my next one-on-one starts, then that's not my problem."

"Ahhh gods," Mich gasped, his hips thrust forward. His eyes fluttered, a soft growl of pleasure echoing through the office. "I…after you left this morning, I ate Lora out. I had to taste her."

I smirked. I had known that would happen and was sad to miss it, but now I got to hear every single detail.

"Every detail," I said. "Every single thing."

His hips thrust forward as I stroked him, working him up. I leaned down and locked eyes with him, flicking my tongue over the head of his cock.

It was like lightning had struck him. His entire body reacted as he bit down, fighting off a cry as pleasure burned through him.

I took the head of his cock between my lips, still stroking him.

"I started with her clit," he gasped out. "She was still warm and sleepy next to me, and I pulled her close, reaching down to play with her. She was already wet and needy, and I wanted to make her cum more. She deserves all the orgasms."

I smiled a little and then went back to sucking, enjoying this torture.

"Ahhh," he gasped, his hands curling into fists.

His claws raked over the desk, his little growls music to my ears.

He was trying so hard for me.

"So I played with her clit and then spread her legs. I moved down my bed and started to lick her. She likes my tongue."

I pulled off his cock for a moment with a chuckle. "I'm sure she does."

Mich laughed a little, but it was cut off by another groan. "She came on my tongue, and she tasted like heaven. And then the two of us got ready for work. We talked about you and how much we want you."

He was holding something back, and so I paused everything, looking up at him.

"Every detail," I snarled.

He lifted his head, his eyes widening.

I glared. "What else did you say, Mich?"

"Nothing bad," he whispered.

"Slave," I warned. "Tell me. Now."

"We're worried about you," Mich said, his voice dropping. "You're hiding something, and it's obvious. We aren't humans, you know. The way you left work yesterday and some of the comments you've made make us wonder."

Well, I wasn't going to win actor of the year for sure. It wasn't just Inferna that was picking up on something, but Mich and Lora too.

"I just want to know you're okay," Mich whispered.

"I will be," I said, stroking him again. "What else did you do?"

Mich's expression fell as he realized I wasn't budging,

but the pleasure coursing through him distracted him enough to help him forget.

I wanted to tell him everything.

But no.

Not yet.

I couldn't put another person in danger like this ever again.

# performance

## MICH

I WANTED TO FIGHT WHATEVER DEMONS WERE haunting my Master, but I couldn't bring myself to keep thinking about it when their hand was wrapped around my cock.

They took my entire length down their throat, damn near sending me over the edge.

"And then I came up the elevator and ran into you," I gasped, finishing everything about my day.

Cinder's mouth was fucking heaven. Everything about it was perfect, from the rhythm they sucked me to the things their tongue did.

I was so close to cumming again. I was even desperate to. This rut was driving me insane.

I was constantly hiding my hard-on. At one point, I'd even wanted to grind against my desk because I was so fucking horny.

It didn't help that Lora was a tease. She'd gone home

and changed and then showed up at the office wearing a black lace dress.

No one would know but me and Cinder that she wasn't wearing underwear.

Cinder sucked me harder, and I gasped, my claws raking into the tabletop.

"I'm so close, Master," I rasped. "Please let me cum."

Cinder continued, raking their fingers down my chest. I groaned, desperate to cum. Desperate to fill their mouth.

I thrust up, hitting the back of their throat. Cinder let out a soft groan and I closed my eyes.

Cinder suddenly pulled back, surprising me. "Fuck. Get up," they whispered.

Panic flew through me at the thought of someone walking in.

"Hurry, someone is coming. I'll intercept them."

Fuck! I could barely think straight.

Cinder gave me a devilish look and then shook their head, moving towards the door. They opened it quickly and then shut it quickly, leaving me scrambling.

My heart pounded in my chest, my cock throbbing. It was standing straight up, the spurs quivering with need. My knot pulsed painfully, threatening me.

I heard voices and slid off the desk, reaching for my pants just as the door flew open.

I let out a small yelp, but it didn't matter. I stared in shock as Lora was shoved in, followed by Cinder and the office door slamming.

"I swore I wasn't going to risk anything," Cinder hissed.

Lora's eyebrows shot up, and she turned, looking straight at me. Her eyes fell down to my throbbing cock, the pens and pencils on the floor, the scattered papers, and the claw marks on the desk.

"Oh I see," Lora said, snorting. "And you're doing really good at that."

"Shut up," Cinder hissed, but they grinned. "Did you come up for your one-on-one?"

"Yes," Lora said, her eyes widening.

"Good. Get on your knees and finish him while I get some stuff together. I have ideas. You said you like pain, right?"

"Yes," she whispered, biting her bottom lip.

"Good. Finish him, pet. You interrupted us."

Fuck. Lora immediately fell to her knees in front of me, looking up at me with wide eyes. She was so fucking gorgeous, her silver hair in soft curls today and lips painted red.

That red was about to be all over my cock.

She reached out, closing her hand around my shaft. I groaned, my head falling back. She began stroking me, her mouth immediately closing around the head.

I reached down and gripped the back of her head, thrusting forward. I was so close to losing control now, and as her nails dug into my thighs, I finally let go.

I pumped into her mouth and started to cum, a deep growl leaving me as cum shot down her throat. She swallowed every drop, holding me to her as everything inside of me seemed to melt.

For a split second, I was able to breathe without the heavy need to mate overtaking me.

She slowly pulled her lips away, licking them with a little grin. "One-on-one, huh?"

I snorted, taking a step back and leaning against the desk.

"Lora, little pet," Cinder said.

We both turned to look at them. They were loading up

the stapler, their expression devious.

"You said you like pain?" Cinder asked.

"I do," Lora whispered, her eyes widening. "I really do."

Cinder nodded, their violet eyes flashing with heated lust. "Get her up on the desk for me, slave."

"Yes, Master," I said.

I leaned down and picked her up with ease, pausing to give her a much-needed kiss before splaying her out on the desk.

Cinder took a step back from us with a little growl and then pulled off their blazer, tossing it over one of the rolling chairs. I watched hungrily as they undid their belt buckle, the sound of the metal clinking making me harder.

Cinder's movements slowed, torturing me as they slid it off and then undid the button.

"Master," Lora rasped. "Master, I want to please you. Please."

"Oh, you will," they said. "You will."

Anticipation ran through me at the thought of them fucking Lora. I would love to see that, to see her bent over the desk and taking them over and over again.

Cinder slowly unbuttoned their shirt, revealing the hard muscles of their chest. They leaned down, their fingers running over Lora's chest. They felt the patterns of the lace, pausing to swirl their fingertips over where her nipples were.

"I can see in the dark," Cinder whispered. "But we should still turn on the lights for this."

"Yes, Master," I said.

I turned and went to the door, flipping the light switch quickly. I turned back around to see that Cinder had moved in front of Lora's head.

"Head off the side of the desk, little pet," they commanded.

Lora's breath hitched as she moved, allowing her head to hang off the side. She parted her legs, the hem of her dress sliding back and revealing her creamy thighs.

Fuck.

I had known she wasn't wearing underwear but now seeing her in front of me like this, I was reminded.

"Eat her out like you did this morning," Cinder said. "I'm going to use her throat and mark her body as mine. And if she needs me to stop, she will make this symbol."

Cinder showed her the symbol, and Lora nodded. "I'll use it if I need to," she said, licking her lips again.

Cinder leaned down, capturing her mouth for a moment. Their kiss made my cock harder, seeing how deeply they devoured each other.

"Beautiful," Cinder said softly, straightening their back.

They slid their black pants down and then their violet thong. Their sex was let free, and Lora moaned, eager to take it down her throat.

Cinder raised their gaze, meeting mine. "I told you to eat her out while I'm fucking her throat and marking her."

"Yes, Master," I whispered.

I leaned down, breathing in her scent. She smelled like heaven, even though she was a hell-born fae. I ran my tongue down her inner thigh, listening to her breath hitch.

I lowered my face to her pussy and then spread her wide with my claws, letting out a long groan.

She was so fucking perfect, and she was mine. Mine to eat. Mine to make cum.

I looked up just as Cinder started to unbutton the top of Lora's dress. She leaned up for a moment, allowing the top part to slide down her body.

"Stunning," Cinder murmured, reaching around to cup one of her breasts. "Isn't she?"

"She is," I whispered reverently.

"I'm going to make you cry, my beautiful little demon. And if you need me to stop, I will stop. Okay?"

"Yes, Master," she said. "I'm yours. I'm yours to do with what you want. And I'm Mich's to make cum."

"Good little pet," Cinder said. "This is a one-on-one you will never forget."

CHAPTER TEN

## *staples*

LORA

My nipples hardened as my bra was tossed to the floor. Cinder cupped the back of my neck for a moment before lowering my head off the side of the desk.

The blood started to rush to my head as I opened my mouth, parting my lips for their sex. They tasted perfect, filling my mouth and then throat as they thrust forward.

Pain shocked me as they slapped my breasts, causing me to gasp. I choked but was immediately assuaged with a moan as Mich buried his tongue inside of me.

My body jerked, but Mich held me down, gripping me so I couldn't writhe away as he began to fuck me with his manticore tongue.

Cinder groaned, giving a little thrust. My head swam as they slapped my other breast, pain followed by pleasure rolling through me.

Fuck. I wanted this so badly. To be used and tormented and even hurt. The pain felt *good*.

Cinder pulled free, and I dragged in air as they lifted my head, groaning. Black tears streamed down my cheeks, and one of their hands came around, covering my mouth as they lifted the stapler with the other.

"You're going to wear what I give you all day," Cinder whispered, their grip tightening. "And then after work, we will take them out and heal you. Have sex, eat, and cuddle."

More tears blurred my vision.

Did they know how badly I wanted this?

I groaned as Mich kept going, sending me straight to the edge.

"That's my good girl," Cinder purred.

I grunted, shivering against them as they leaned in closer. My upper back was now propped against their chest. One of their hands cupped my breast, rolling it in their grip. A little moan left me, my entire body pulsing now with pleasure.

They held the stapler to the breast they held, the cold of the metal making me squeal. Cinder paused for a moment, giving my collarbone a gentle kiss.

"Are you going to be good for your Master?"

"Yes," I whispered.

The anticipation was killing me. All of the sensations building together, driving me insane.

"You can cum more than once," Cinder said, toying with the position of the stapler. They opened it so that it lay flat against my skin, the stark red metal gleaming in the office lighting. "Look at Mich."

I looked down between my legs to where my manticore coworker was devouring me. My hips kept trying to arch up, but he still kept me pinned.

His eyes locked with mine, and I groaned.

"Here we go," Cinder said.

My breath hitched as the sound of the stapler against my skin registered, followed by the stinging pain. I gasped, writhing between the two of them. It burned, but fuck...

Mich moaned, pulling his tongue free for a moment. "You just got so much wetter."

The pain turned me on. I still held his gaze as he began to fuck me with his tongue again.

Cinder adjusted the stapler again, clicking it. The flare of pain engulfed me, but this time it was echoed by an orgasm.

Pleasure crashed through me, and I screamed. Cinder clamped their hand over my mouth, muffling the sound. Tears blurred my vision from the intense waves rolling through my body, everything bursting with the feeling of ecstasy.

The stapler pierced me again and then again and again. I bucked against them, a sob leaving me.

I didn't want them to stop.

Cinder paused for a moment, but I shook my head wildly. "Don't stop. Please," I begged.

"Such a good little pet," Cinder purred. "Look down. Look at the first letter."

I looked down, my pussy still pulsing as Mich cleaned me up.

M.

Cinder had stapled the letter M on me.

"The first letter out of four," Cinder said.

My mind swirled as they held the stapler back to my skin. It was angry and red around the staples I'd already taken, the pain lingering but becoming cathartic.

*Click.*

*Click.*

*Click.*

*Click.*

Cinder moved quickly, working with Mich to hold me in place as they made the next letter. I stopped hearing the noises I was making, sinking so far into my mind that all I could feel was the safety of being with them. All I knew was pain and pleasure, the two feelings dancing together like wild mates.

*Click. Click. Click. Click. Click.*

I arched against them, a second orgasm crashing into me. Cinder's hand covered my mouth, containing my ragged scream. My chest heaved with breaths, my legs trembling as Mich still lapped at me.

"She tastes so good," Mich moaned.

"She's perfect," Cinder praised. "Last letter, little pet. You've been such a good girl for us. I can't wait for you to see the mark."

I couldn't even form words, so I just nodded. Black tears rolled down my cheeks, only to be swiped away gently.

"One more, little pet," Cinder crooned. "Can you do it for me?"

"Yes, Master," I rasped.

*Click. Click. Click. Click. Click. Click.*

I counted every single one of them, my fingers digging into the desktop.

*Click. Click. Click.*

"Last one."

I let out a shuddering cry as the last staple went in. *Click.*

"Gooood," Cinder hummed. "Lovely. Take a look."

I opened my eyes, wiping away the tears and looking down at the work Cinder had done.

MINE.

They had truly marked me as theirs.

"Oh," I whispered, "Master."

There was something about it. Something about being told  I was theirs, that I belonged to them. My vision was already blurry, but more tears filled my eyes, and I felt my throat tighten.

Cinder let out a gentle sigh and leaned down, wrapping their arms around me and holding me to them. Mich raised his head, watching the two of us with a soft smile.

"Mine," Cinder murmured, stroking my face.

"Yours," I agreed.

Fuck.

It had been too long since I had felt like this, and it was overwhelming. Overwhelming, but...

It felt right.

The two of them felt right.

I felt that tug again, the one that told me I truly did belong with them. The one I'd been fighting. I had worked so hard to become completely independent, to get away from a terrible relationship that had hurt me.

Monsters fell in love easily, especially if there were heats and ruts involved. Sometimes it was hard to see if they were really the right one, but this felt different.

Cinder reached up and traced the word with their fingertip. "How are you feeling?"

"Good," I whispered. "That was intense. I think I'm falling in love with both of you."

Fuck. The words were out of my mouth before I realized what I had said. Both Mich and Cinder tensed up, and I started to move, only to be held in place. Cinder's arms tightened, and Mich let out a soft growl.

"No, you can't run after saying that," Mich chuckled.

"No, you can't," Cinder agreed.

"Sorry," I whispered. "I don't want to make things weird—"

"Things have already gotten weird," Mich said, standing. "But... who cares? I feel it too."

I wiped away a tear and let out a sigh, closing my eyes.

Being vulnerable was hard. Being honest was hard.

But with the two of them, it was safe.

I was about to say something else when Cinder made a noise, looking at the door. "Get dressed."

Fuck.

The three of us moved quickly, getting dressed and getting everything back in place. The sound of footsteps echoed down the hall, along with a couple of voices.

Cinder lunged for the door, flipping off the light switch. They held their finger to their lips, the three of us falling deadly silent.

The muffled voices became clearer, the words distinguishable.

"The HR agent. I don't think he will do what needs to be done. It's up to the two of us," a voice said.

"Shhh," the other hissed. "You don't know if we're in the clear. We have to make sure no one is here before we talk. And we only have a moment before Alex comes back."

"We need to report to Hazard that Cinder has already fucked up."

Cinder tensed, their expression turning unreadable. I felt my stomach fall, my heart pounding in my chest.

What were they talking about?

"The only way we can take this office back is by getting rid of Alex."

"There's no way without getting rid of Inferna and Art first. They're both too on top of things. And now that they are aware of some of the things happening, it makes it harder."

I looked at Mich, and the misery there was enough to make my stomach twist again.

We had been right.

Cinder was part of them. Whomever they were. The ones that had attacked us, that were hurting the omega witches.

But why? Why was this happening?

Their words became muffled again and then stopped, their presence disappearing as they either went to the elevator or down the stairs.

Silence settled over the three of us, and then I felt the cracks in the numbness. Anger flashed through me, and a growl left me.

Cinder was frozen in place, their chest moving as their breaths came faster.

"Cinder," I growled. "What the fuck?!"

They made a noise, looking up at me. I marched straight up to them, going toe to toe. I could feel the darkness creeping up, crowding my vision.

"Lora," Mich growled.

I'd just fucking told them I was falling in love with them, and now this?!

"What the fuck was that?" I screeched.

Cinder flinched, and that somehow hurt more than anything they had done to me today or yesterday.

Burly hands settled on my hips, and I was pulled back from Cinder by Mich, his arms wrapping around me.

"I thought you were in trouble," Mich said. "Not that you were one of them."

"I..." Cinder drifted off, making another noise. "Fuck. If I tell you both the truth, it could hurt both of you."

Tears filled my eyes, my chest hurting now. Not from the staples but from the sense of betrayal.

"I think we're already hurt," I whispered.

Cinder opened their mouth to speak, but then the sound of voices came again. This time, they were much more familiar.

Inferna and Alex.

Fuck.

"I will explain after work," Cinder said. "I promise."

"If you don't, I'm sending you straight to hell," I sneered.

"*Lora*," Mich said.

I shoved him away, still angry. "You weren't the one that was attacked by one of them, Mich. So shut the fuck up. I'm done with both of you for the day, so just leave me alone."

Mich made a noise, but I didn't look back. In fact, I finished buttoning up my dress and then yanked open the door, stepping out into the hall.

Inferna and Alex were down at the end, both looking at me. I gave them a small wave, rushing past them.

"One-on-one was great. What a great HR person we have," I lied, cutting around the corner before either one of them could get a word in.

The staples on my chest spelled out 'mine', but I felt like I'd just been abandoned all over again.

"Lora!"

I froze in my tracks at Inferna's voice, turning to see her walking towards me. She made a face as she got closer, nodding her head for me to walk with her.

"Is there something you need?" I asked.

"Yes," Inferna said. "But let's get to the elevator."

Fuck. I was trying my best to mask my feelings, to the

point of it hurting. I followed after Inferna, the two of us waiting for the elevator doors to open.

We stepped inside, and as they shut, she turned and looked at me. "What happened?"

"I don't want to talk about it," I said. "In fact, I want to go home for the day. I'm not feeling well."

Inferna was quiet for a moment and then nodded. "Okay. I will let Art know."

My muscles relaxed some, and I fought back tears.

"All people are idiots sometimes," Inferna said. "I don't know what happened, but you can always talk to me."

"I know," I whispered. "Why is being a monster so hard?"

Inferna's expression softened. "It sucks sometimes."

"I just want to be loved," I whispered.

"Oh, Lora," Inferna sighed. "Fuck. Now I'm going to end up firing both of them."

"No, don't do that," I said, smiling a little.

Inferna would too.

"It's fine. It'll be fine."

"Well, go home and take a bubble bath. Maybe some hell salts and bubbles? Order some food and forget about work."

I nodded. "Thank you," I said, giving her a little smile.

"Always," she said.

The doors to the elevator opened, and we both stepped out. I gave her a nod and went down the hall, through the office, and to our tables.

I grabbed my bag and didn't even spare Calen a glance. I was too fucking mad and barely hanging on by a thread.

I rushed back through the office, ignoring the swiveling heads. I made it to the elevators, my heart giving a little flutter as the elevator doors slid open.

Cinder and Mich were standing there, and before I could argue, I was pulled inside as the doors shut.

"Let me go!" I yelled.

"Lora, please," Cinder said. "Please let me explain what's going on."

"I don't want anything to do with either one of you right now," I growled.

"Lora—"

That was it. I felt the darkness inside of me break like a storm unleashing a torrent of rain. Cinder and Mich both hit the walls of the elevator, and it came to a screeching halt, the lights flickering as my darkness pinned them in place.

Cinder shoved forward, their magic sparking with violet flares of light, but it didn't matter. I pushed them back, stepping up close.

I bared my fangs, my talons sharp and wings ready.

"You have less than one minute," I hissed. "Less than one minute to make this right."

# aftercare

## CINDER

I had underestimated how powerful Lora was.

I had also underestimated how caught up I was in everything with her and Mich. She said she was falling in love, but I was already fucking there.

There wasn't anything I could do about that.

But, I could try to take the hurt away from her burning eyes.

The elevator rattled, the lights still flickering. Mich let out a soft grunt, trying to fight the cloud of inky black that had him pinned to the wall.

"My sister is an omega witch," I said. "And a few years ago, the company that controls everything here tried to take her. So to keep that from happening, I agreed to work for them. And I have," I whispered, tears blurring my vision. "I have. I've done bad things. And I'm sorry. I was sent here after Alice died, and I didn't expect to meet the two of you. Hell, it hasn't even been forty-eight hours, and I've felt more than I ever have for anyone. And I'm fighting it because I'm scared that if I mess up, Ember will die."

Lora stared at me for a moment, and I felt the grip of her darkness slowly loosen. Between the flicker of the lights was her darkness and the glow of my purple magic illuminating the three of us.

Mich growled, and Lora let him go, her gaze never leaving mine. My eyes darted to him, making sure he was okay.

"Lora," Mich said, bending over for a moment to catch his breath. "Lora, you're going to end up hurting them. I know you're mad but it's going to be okay. We're going to talk through everything. Cinder is being honest."

Lora finally let me go. I fell forward, but she caught me, surprising me by wrapping her arms around my neck.

That broke me.

My knees buckled, and I hit the ground in front of her, all of the weight and worry from the last few years pulling me down. She held on to me, though, holding me to her.

Even though I had hurt her.

Even though I had hurt Mich.

"Get us out of here," Lora whispered. "You're a witch. Just take us to my apartment."

My magic wasn't the best with portals, but I still nodded. I reached out, and Mich took my hand, and then I closed my eyes— drawing a path with my mind.

I whispered a spell and felt my magic open up, swallowing the three of us and then dumping us straight into her apartment.

I opened my eyes, leaning back and looking around.

Lora sat back and sighed. Mich gave the two of us a gentle look, his honey-colored eyes a little sad.

"We'll worry about work later," Mich said. "I'm sure Inferna will keep quiet."

Lora nodded. "She's good."

The silence settled between us, and I felt my anxiety grow. I'd just let out my biggest secret, and it was scary to think that I didn't have to handle it alone.

"I'm going to go take a bath," Lora whispered. "And then the three of us can talk about...everything."

I nodded as Lora stood, leaving Mich and me alone in her living room.

We were both silent as the sound of water started, echoing around us. I held my breath for a moment, trying not to shut down. This had turned into so much more, and I wished I could go back in time.

"Do you regret us?" Mich whispered.

My head snapped up, and I looked at my manticore. Mine. Just as much as Lora was mine.

"No," I whispered, moving towards him. I reached out and pulled him close, sliding my hands into his rough palms. "I don't regret you," I said. "I don't regret Lora. I just regret the circumstances."

Mich nodded, his eyes falling down. "All of this has moved fast, but I wouldn't want it any other way. And even though I can barely think past my cock right now, I still knew something was wrong."

"It's complicated," I said.

"But you're not alone now," Mich said, looking back up at me. "You're not alone, Cinder. And even though Lora is angry right now, she's not done either."

I nodded, pressing my lips together.

"Also, holy fuck. She's a little frightening."

I snorted, smiling. "She is. She is very powerful."

"I know that if she ever sings, we're in danger," Mich said, giving my hands a squeeze.

"Well, hopefully she never has to sing," I said, finally looking around her apartment.

It was small but cozy and covered with art supplies. Her kitchen table was behind the couch, and there were countless balls of yarn, crocheting needles, and a couple of forgotten mugs of tea.

"I didn't know she crocheted," I said.

"Well, you did meet her yesterday," Mich teased.

True. Our lives had really taken a turn since Monday morning.

Mich pulled me to standing, and then I tugged him close, pulling him down into a kiss. He let out a moan, melting against me.

For a tough manticore, he was really just a teddy bear that wanted to be loved.

"We should order some food for the three of us, and I should probably call Inferna," I said. "And come up with some reason as to why I disappeared."

"Tell her that your sister needs you," Mich said, already rummaging for his phone in his pocket. "That's not a lie. And yeah, I wouldn't lie to Inferna, honestly. She's the best, but she's tough. Art is good too, so you could call him. He's just as fierce, although Inferna is something else. I will order some food," Mich said.

"Thank you," I said, moving towards the couch.

I plopped on the cushion and damn near fell into another dimension but managed to readjust myself despite Mich's laughter.

"Good gods," I muttered, shaking my head.

I pulled up Inferna's number and decided to text her instead.

The other problem was I was being watched now, and no one would see me leave work today. This would start some rumors.

I needed to call my sister after.

Hi Inferna. I had a family emergency and had to leave. I will be back tomorrow.

Inferna's response was almost immediate.

**Inferna**: Hope everything is okay. If you need anything, just call. I have connections and you're not alone.

The succubus had to be psychic. I sighed and leaned my head back, listening to Mich call in the food. He ordered half the menu and then hung up, turning to look at me.

I patted the couch cushion next to me. "Come cuddle until our lady comes back."

Mich sat next to me, and the couch groaned, making both of us stare down at it like it was its own creature.

"We can't fuck on this little thing," Mich said.

I laughed, finally feeling a break in the pressure weighing me down. "No, we'd have to get her a new couch."

Mich thought about this for a moment and then grinned. "Okay. Well, maybe we do fuck on it and break it."

"You'd like that," I teased, leaning against him.

The two of us sat there for a few minutes, silence settling over us. I could hear his heartbeat and the sound of water as Lora moved in the bathtub.

"So, your sister," Mich murmured. "Tell me about her."

"Well," I said, relaxing.

How did I describe Ember?

"She's magical," I said. "A very strong witch. We've had

a rough road but have always stuck together. The omega thing wasn't an issue until she turned eighteen. Then it happened. But... she is a wonderful person. Kind, smart, and sassy. A little angry at the world and sometimes scared, but that's never stopped her."

"I imagine it's scary," Mich said. "I've never had to worry about creatures attacking me. Only humans."

I nodded. "Humans...well, most witches can walk around humans, and they won't know the difference. And many monsters have their human forms that allow it, but it's still difficult."

"It's very uncomfortable," Mich said. "It feels like you're being shoved into a tiny box and suffocating. But for a moment, it allows you to be out in the world without fear."

The sound of water splashing echoed through the apartment, and we both looked towards the doorway. Within a few moments, Lora walked in, wearing nothing but a purple towel with little demons on it.

Mich and I were both silent as we watched her, waiting like beggars as she ignored us, went to the kitchen and poured water, and then went back to her room.

Mich let out a hiss. "She's..."

"Stunning," I mumbled.

Mine. She was mine. She was ours.

Fuck.

Lora came back wearing a short silky black shift, her short silver hair damp. All of her makeup had been washed off, and her wings lounged behind her, wilted like pretty flower petals.

The staples were still on her skin, catching the light.

"I can remove them," I said.

Lora hesitated for a moment and then nodded. I stood,

offering her my seat. She took it, sinking against Mich as I knelt on the floor in front of her.

"I liked it," Lora said.

I nodded, drawing on my magic. I used it to pluck the staples out, making it quick so it didn't sting too much. Lora winced a couple of times, but between Mich's never-ending comfort and my magic, it was done within a few moments.

I grabbed all the staples and took them to the kitchen, dumping them in the trash before returning.

Lora gave me a little smile and then arched a brow. "So. Spill it all. What's this company doing with omega witches? Why are they focusing on this office?"

"I don't know why they're focusing on this office," I said, pressing my lips together.

Mich shuffled over on the couch and patted the seat between the two of them.

"If I sit there, I'm going to end up in one of the circles of hell."

Lora and Mich both laughed.

"Oh, come on," Lora said. "If you do, I'll bring you back."

I gave her a doubtful look but joined them anyways, sinking between the cushions. The three of us were effectively shoved together, and Lora even leaned her head on my shoulder, which felt like a peace offering.

"I don't know everything, but this ring of criminals runs deep," I said. "And for the last few years, I've been working for them to keep my sister safe. Most of it has just been office work. They've moved me around the country and have had me keep an ear to the ground. I've done...I've done a lot. I'm one of their best. Others trust me easily, and so I've used that to my advantage. I think Alex knows."

"Hmm... I can't say that either of us knows him very

well. But he was rescued when Art and Inferna rescued Calen. Art was kidnapped from my understanding, but all of it has kind of been glossed over," Mich said.

"Alex also incinerated a vampire and a witch," Lora mumbled.

"Oh yeah," Mich said. "Gods. Yeah, he's got some crazy magic."

"He's very powerful," I said. "Probably old as dirt. The older a witch is, the more powerful they become. But.... essentially, there are monsters and witches involved in this. I don't know what they need the omegas for, but...."

"Maybe for breeding," Lora said, shivering next to me. "I can't stand the thought of it, but it would make sense. Omegas are supposedly rare, right? For witches, anyway. So finding all of them and keeping them...well. Why else would you want someone?"

"Humans do things like this to their own kind, and it's atrocious," Mich whispered. "Trafficking."

My stomach twisted at the thought, tears filling my eyes.

"Where is your sister right now?" Lora asked.

"She's at our current home on the east side."

"Maybe we should get her somewhere else."

"We can't," I said, "They're always watching. They will know if she is taken."

"What if...." Lora drifted off. "What if she was kidnapped?"

"What?" I asked, sitting up some.

"I mean, Inferna has connections. We could stage a kidnapping, so they think you have nothing to do with it."

"And then what? She goes and hides somewhere else, and I have to pretend? There's no way out of this for us, and there hasn't been for years."

"You were alone before," Mich said. "You're not now."

"Tomorrow, we should talk to Inferna and Art. Without Alex," Lora said. She looked up at me, her eyes pleading. "Please let others help you for once."

Fuck. How could I say no?

A knock at the door had us all looking up, and then Mich got up. "Food," he said.

"Ah, yes," I said.

Mich went to the door and opened it, grabbing all the bags of food.

"Oh god," Lora giggled as he kicked the door shut. "How much did you order?"

"I'm a big boy, and I've been active today," he said, carrying it all to the kitchen.

Lora started to stand, but I grabbed her hand, turning her to look at me. "Lora, I'm sorry. I'm sorry for hurting you. Mich asked me if I regretted you and him, and I don't. I want you to know that. I just...I'm tired of causing people pain."

She stared at me for a moment and then leaned down, brushing her lips over mine. I groaned a little, feeling a rush of relief and need all at once.

"I forgive you," she whispered. "I understand why you did what you did. It was just...I have my own problems. And at some point, I should probably talk about them. But it reminded me of my ex and how he used to manipulate and lie to me. And that hurt."

"That's valid," I said earnestly. "I would like to hear about that...when you're ready."

She gave me a soft smile and cupped my cheek. "Come eat, Cinder. We're going to spend the rest of the day planning. And then tomorrow, we'll go in ready to fight."

With that, she drew back and then went to the kitchen.

I watched as she gave Mich a big hug from behind, giggling as she held on to him like a koala while he unpacked the food.

There was a little bit of freedom on the horizon, and now I had hope.

Hope that this could be my life. That Ember could live her own too.

Hope that all of the monsters waiting in the dark wouldn't devour us.

# hump day murderers

## MICH

I STEPPED INTO THE OFFICE AT 9 A.M., READY TO FIGHT.

Knowing everything that I did now, everyone in the office was now labeled an enemy. Even Anne at the front desk until I knew otherwise.

The only people we were certain were good were the three that had been affected directly by everything recently. Inferna, Calen, and Art. Even Alex was suspicious.

The fact that my mate— my mate— had been living under this curse for so long made me furious.

"Good morning, Mich," Anne called.

I gave her a little wave, heading straight for Art's office.

We had a plan today. A plan to make sure that we could get Ember to safety.

Well, if everything went correctly.

I glanced across the office to where Cinder sat, pretending to work already.

Lora was going to Inferna, I was going to Art, and then we would go from there.

I gave a short knock on the doorframe and then peeked my head in. Art was drinking a cup of coffee out of his infamous 'Witches Get Bitches' mug, one that he had hidden from Cinder.

He turned, surprised. "Good morning, Mich."

"Morning. Do you have a minute?" I asked.

Art nodded. "Of course. Come in."

I shut the door behind me and let out a breath, not knowing where to begin.

"I have a request," I said, looking around the office nervously. "But I need to write it down."

Art scowled and then nodded. "Okay."

He pulled out a sticky notepad and a pen, sliding them across his desk. I wrote out my note quickly, feeling the back of my neck prickle.

Can you put up a spell of silence? I have something to discuss, but don't know if someone else can hear.

Art read it, arched a brow, and then nodded. "Would you like a cup of coffee?"

"Yes," I said.

It was a dance, the two of us pretending that everything was normal. Art went to his coffee pot, one that Inferna had gifted him recently, and poured a new cup. He brought it over to me and, as he set it down, spoke the spell.

I could feel the magic spread through the room and let out a breath, relaxing.

"What the fuck is going on?" Art asked, arching a dark brow.

"Everything," I said. "A whole ass shit show. Cinder was an agent sent by that company to infiltrate the office, but they're not actually bad. They've been forced into it because of their sister. Their sister is an omega witch, and the only way they could keep her from being dragged into all of this was by joining them."

"For fuck's sake," Art groaned, sitting in his chair. "I knew it. I fucking knew it. Calen owes me ten dollars."

"Hey, don't bet on my mate," I grumbled.

"Your MATE?" Art asked, leaning forward. "Good god. Inferna was right. Fuck, now I owe her ten dollars."

"Why were you betting on us?"

"Listen, I know I'm not a monster, but I still have eyes. The three of you have sex written all over your faces. I can't smell it, but I can fucking see it," Art said.

I blinked, shaking my head. "It's not my fault I fell into a rut."

Art held up a hand. "I don't care why and I'd rather not know the details. But...okay, so what now?"

"We need help getting Ember somewhere safe. We want to stage her being kidnapped. Ember is Cinder's sister," I said. "And she's currently being held at their home. But Cinder is worried that once that happens, all hell will break loose."

Art nodded. "Cinder would be correct. These guys are bad."

"They are," I agreed, sighing. "I just want Cinder to be safe. I'm concerned. And I don't trust anyone now. Not with Hazard disappearing after everything, and then we overheard two people talking yesterday, and I couldn't place their voices. But there are spies in the office."

"Well, let me get Inferna," Art said.

"I think Lora is already talking to her. We were trying not to draw attention by all of us meeting."

Art paused and scowled. "Fuck. Good point. Hmm.

Maybe we will pretend to have a performance meeting with all of you."

"That could work, but there are still other people in the office," I said.

"Hmm. Maybe we could get dinner after work then," Art said, glancing up at the clock.

I was about to respond when the door flew open, and Inferna and Lora stepped in.

"Inferna," Art said, standing.

"Meeting," Inferna said. "Get Cinder and Calen. Call it a secret project from corporate. Go to the shifting room, it's safe."

Before anyone could respond, Inferna turned on her heels.

Lora gave me a quick look and then smiled, following after her.

"Well," Art said. "Never mind then. To the shifting room. I'll go get Cinder and Calen."

THE SIX OF US ALL STOOD IN THE DARK, GATHERED IN A circle like we were about to summon the evilest demon and not like we were at the office on a chilly Wednesday.

Calen and Art put up a spell, one that would keep every prying eye and ear away from us while we talked.

"Okay," Inferna said. "Lora filled me in."

"Mich filled me in," Art said.

"I have no idea what's going on," Calen said, looking around.

"Basically, Cinder needs our help. Now. Cinder," Inferna said, looking at them. "How deep does this circle run?"

"Deep," Cinder answered, grimacing. They raked their

fingertips through their dark hair, biting their lower lip. "I don't know who is who, either. That's the problem. But I know that the main boss stays in the building across the street and is always having us watched. I don't know why this office, in particular, is of such importance, but it is. Important enough that they immediately sent me in even after Alice was killed. They have only sent their best too. Alice had done a lot and was high up on the chain. Hazard too."

Silence settled over us as we finally registered what we had believed. Hazard had been bad.

That probably meant that Poppins was too.

Lora shook her head, crossing her arms. "I just don't understand why they would do this. Creatures already have to work through terrible things. And now we're trying to come out in the world more."

"It's awful," Calen whispered. There was a tone of knowing in his voice, a reminder that he had seen more than us.

"It is," Inferna agreed. "Well. How comfortable with murder is everyone here?"

"Inferna!" Art exclaimed.

Her question had all of us looking around like crazy people, but I was the first to say it straight.

"Listen, all of us are monsters," I said. "All of us have done things, I'm sure. I'm still young for a manticore, but I've still been around for a century. Things happen."

"We can't justify murder," Lora hissed.

Inferna and I both made faces, which weren't well received by the witches.

"I ask because I know someone," Inferna said. "And this could get bad fast if things go sideways. I ask because I like to prepare everyone for what could happen. We might have to fight some bad people, and they might end up dead. Art and I definitely...dealt with some bad guys while saving Calen."

"If I have to murder someone who has been torturing omega witches in order to keep them from hurting my mate and their sister, then so be it," I said, shrugging.

Lora made a noise, followed by Calen, who had paled significantly.

"Don't worry," Art said. "Hopefully, it won't come to that. But...we are trying to keep an eye on who we think is a spy. We could use that knowledge to our advantage if we're smart. You said you heard two people come upstairs? Was that before Alex and Inferna did? I could look back at cameras."

"Already tried," Inferna said. "They were using shielding magic."

"Great," Art sighed. "Alright. First, we need to rescue your sister and get her out of harm's way. Then we need to deal with the aftermath and make sure you don't get hurt. Maybe you should go with her, Cinder."

The thought of Cinder being away from Lora and me made my chest ache.

"No," Cinder said. "I won't leave Lora and Mich. Plus... if we're together, then we are easier to track."

Inferna looked up, glancing at the door. "We don't have too much longer, but Cinder— I need your address, and then I need you to very obviously leave and go somewhere after work tonight. Somewhere that would make them follow you, potentially."

"They can come over to my place," Lora said. "We can have a movie night."

Inferna smirked, her tail swishing behind her. "Right. Alright then."

Art pointed at Calen. "You lost the bet."

"Damn it," Calen muttered, reaching into his back pocket and pulling out his wallet.

He pulled out a bill and started to hand it to Art, but Inferna plucked it with a satisfied hum. "Ah yes, and you lost yours too, dear Art."

Art rolled his eyes but didn't hide his grin. "Dramatic."

"Dramatic and twenty dollars richer."

We all laughed. I took a deep breath, looking over at Cinder. They were barely smiling, their worry obvious. I reached out, placing my hand on their shoulder.

"It's going to be okay," I said softly.

Cinder nodded. "Okay. Well, the other thing is I have no way of telling my sister."

"She'll be okay," Inferna said. "I'm sending some family. She will be safe and staying with a werewolf, werecat, and their human. And no one will mess with them unless they want to meet death. I can guarantee that."

Cinder let out a relieved sigh. "Okay. Thank you all for helping me. I don't know...I don't know why you are helping me. But I am thankful."

"No one deserves to be treated the way they treated those witches," Inferna said. "And also, you work for me now."

"That means that if someone disrupts the flow of things, which includes endangering employees, then Inferna is ready to kill," Art teased.

Inferna smirked and shrugged. "I am the boss, even though Alex thinks he is."

"It's true," Lora giggled.

I smiled at her.

Everything would be okay. It had to be.

"Alright, creatures," Inferna said. "We need to get back

out on the floor. And Calen and Art need a break from spellcasting. Also, to help break up any rumors, Cinder—you can come work upstairs with Alex and me. And maybe actually get the one on ones done."

"Sounds like a plan," Cinder said.

With that, we all went back to work.

## CHAPTER THIRTEEN

## LORA

Cinder and I moved across the parking garage, trying not to look around us like we were paranoid.

It was getting harder to act like everything was normal when I knew any one of our coworkers could be working for some really evil bastards.

The work day had crept by slowly, but we were finally done and able to go home. Mich was going to meet us at my apartment, and I was going to ride with Cinder.

It was trouble. We all knew that. But at some point, we'd decided we were in this together.

I ran the tip of my tongue over my fangs, thinking about my witch. They were meant to be my mate, just like Mich was. And I had finally started to let that thought sink in.

Last night, after the three of us had talked for a while, I had realized a few things.

One, I was definitely in love with the two of them already.

Two, this was right. It felt different. The bonds that had already formed were ones I couldn't simply leave. I wanted this.

Three, we had the chance to help more creatures that were trapped by this evil company.

I wanted to know why they did this to others. I wanted to know what evil bastard sat at the top pulling all the strings.

Hopefully, we would learn. Hopefully, we could stop them.

Cinder and I got into their car and they started it, pulling out of the parking garage.

Was it my paranoia telling me that we were being watched? I leaned against the door, peering out the window and up at the building across from ours.

I couldn't see them, but I felt them.

The back of my neck prickled. Anger rushed through me as Cinder turned onto the busy street, the sun already starting to set.

I ran my tongue over my fangs.

I wanted to mate with Cinder and with Mich. I wanted the three of us to seal these bonds, to make what we wanted come true.

I ached for them both.

"I can feel them," I whispered.

"Yes," Cinder said, glancing in the rearview. "They're watching. Wondering. And Inferna swore that they were already working on grabbing my sister?"

"Yes," I said, finally tearing my eyes from the ominous building. "We should find out what company owns that place. Maybe then we can figure out more info."

"That would be a good idea," Cinder said.

They were tense, gripping the steering wheel like it was their lifeline.

The last few days had been a lot, but I wouldn't trade it for anything.

Cinder and Mich were mine.

"I want to be mated," I said. "Fully. We already know we have the mated bonds and I want this."

"I want it too," Cinder said.

Their words alone helped break up the nasty storm in my chest. It felt good to hear those words.

To know I wasn't the only one who wanted this.

To know they wanted it too.

That only made my hunger intensify. The thirst to taste their blood, to draw a mark with it on my body. I wanted to feel their tongue on my pussy and Mich's cock down my throat this time.

"Lora," Cinder growled. "Your aura is pulsing with lust. You're distracting me."

"I can't help it," I said. "My entire body is burning, witch."

"Witch," Cinder said, smirking. "You never call me a witch."

"Well, you're a witch tonight. And I'm your demon. Mich will be my sacrifice."

"Hmm, the little demon is hungry."

"I am," I hissed. "I want your blood, witch."

Cinder's lips pulled into a wicked smile. All of the worries from work melted away, the car becoming warmer. They stole a glance, their violet and black eyes holding mine before hitting the road again.

"I think I can allow you to call me that for the evening. Instead of Master."

"Yes," I said. "Get us home quickly."

"So demanding," Cinder whispered. "Is it not witches who summon demons, dear one?"

"Is it not demons that devour witches, mate?"

"Only when we allow it."

"Oh, I think not. I think your magic won't do anything to me the moment I have you in my apartment."

"I have an idea. If you want to play."

"Yes." I looked over at them. "Tell me."

"We can tie  Mich down on your bed and have some fun."

"Hmm." I thought about it. "Is this you getting out of me tying you down?"

"No," Cinder chuckled. "This is me getting you out of punishment for being a brat."

"I want you to fuck me while his monster cock is inside of me. I want to bite into your neck and taste your witch blood and then draw a demon's mark on us to seal our bond. And I want to mate Mich until his rut is finally broken. I want to make him cum until he's begging me to stop. And then I want both of you to fuck me until I can't remember if we're in heaven, hell, or the office."

My words lingered between us, and Cinder smirked, gripping the steering wheel. Patches of light fell on their brown skin from the sunset, highlighting their dark hair and the piercings along their ear and through their eyebrow.

"As you wish, little pet," Cinder said. "I think these are requests I can support."

I bared my fangs at them, and they reached out with one hand, gripping my thigh. They gave me a light squeeze, and I bit back a moan as their palm erupted with pinpricks of magic.

"Don't worry, little demon," Cinder said. "I promise that by the time we go to work tomorrow, you will be mated to me and fucked thoroughly. I can't guarantee that Mich will agree, but I have a feeling he will. And I want him too. I belong to both of you monsters."

I nodded and glanced at the clock.

Only a few more minutes of weaving through traffic and then we would be home.

If the fucking enemies were going to stalk us, watch us, and listen to us— then we might as well put on a show they wouldn't forget. And I might as well finally seal the bond with Cinder and Mich.

# on wednesdays, we sacrifice

Cinder

LORA SHOVED ME AGAINST THE ELEVATOR WALL AS WE rode up to her floor, and I lifted her, spinning her around and slamming her back. Her wings spread behind her, her pussy pulsing with heat against my waist as we kissed.

Fuck. I needed her. I needed Mich. I could barely think about anything else happening with her tongue down my throat, her sharp teeth scraping against my lips.

I tasted blood, and I wasn't sure whose it was, but it made her feral.

My little demon was hungry. Hungry to be bred and fucked senseless.

The doors rang and slid open, and I didn't set her down. In fact, we both ignored the gasp of the human that had been waiting as I carried her down the hall to her door.

Humans were always so easily shocked.

With the flick of my hand, the door flew open, and I carried her inside.

I already smelled Mich. I moved through the apartment, taking Lora all the way to the living room and dropping her on his lap.

"Whoa," Mich gasped, catching her. "Whoa. Both of you are....ah, fuck."

Lora turned in his lap, straddling him and grinding against him as she gripped his fur. I watched as every conceivable thought left our manticore, his eyes damn near rolling to the back of his head.

"Ah fuck," he rasped. "You made it home safe."

"We did," I said, ripping off my jacket.

I undid my tie, watching as Lora and Mich lost each other in a kiss. I started to unbutton my shirt, need rushing through me.

I was just as hungry as she was. I needed to be with them, needed to forget all of our problems.

Lora pulled back with a moan and then stood, gripping Mich's collar and pulling him forward. "We're tying you down to the bed, and I'm mating you. And so is Cinder. Unless you have any objections."

Mich's eyes widened like saucers, his breath hitching. "No, Lora, no objections. I want this. This sounds like a good plan. Are you sure?"

"We're both sure," I growled. "Up. To her bed."

"If we break the bed, then fuck it," Lora said, pulling him to standing.

Mich turned to look at me for a moment, his expression one of surprise and lust. "And I thought I was the one in a rut. Dear goddess."

"No fucking gods here, monster," Lora snapped.

My pet was a switch. I grinned as I followed the two of them to her bedroom.

Mich stood no chance. Lora flipped on her bedroom

light, and we were met with a vibrant neon glow, one that made the three of us look like we were in a club. I could taste her darkness, and fuck— I would drink it with my coffee every morning if I could. There was something about her soft wickedness, something about the way she shoved our bulky manticore down on the mattress like he was nothing and then went to her drawer to rummage for rope.

There was something about her. Whatever it was, it was mine.

I caught Mich's slightly horny and slightly nervous gaze and cocked my head. "You wanted to break your rut, right? To not keep getting hard-ons at work. I know it has to get tiring humping the corners of desks."

"Fuck you," Mich breathed, but his cock was already hardening in his pants.

"Strip. You're ours tonight," I said.

I liked seeing Lora like this as much as I enjoyed stapling the word 'mine' on her breasts.

"Fuck," Mich groaned, but he was already peeling off his work clothes.

I smiled as Lora tossed me a bundle of black rope. "I'm assuming you know how to use this," she said.

I arched a brow, fighting off a laugh. "Of course, pet. Do you?"

"No demon girl in their right mind doesn't know how."

Fair enough.

Lora's bed was built for this, which made me wonder about her. I winked at Mich as I tugged one of his ankles toward one of the corners. I unraveled the rope and started to bind him down, all while Lora worked on his wrists.

"Do I get a say in this?" Mich asked, lifting his head helplessly.

"No," Lora said. "Use your safeword if you want to stop, but other than that, no. I'm hungry, manticore."

"I can tell," he said, staring at her in awe.

We were both a little star-struck by our dainty demon mate.

I finished tying down Mich and then looked at her. "What else do you have in that drawer?"

"Take a look," she said. "We haven't really had a chance to be here much, hmm?"

Aside from last night, which hadn't been nearly as kinky. There were times just having nice sex was more than enough, and then there were times like this.

Times where I wanted to use everything I could imagine on my willing victims.

"I will look in a moment," I said, stepping up behind her. "First, I want to undress you. And I want Mich to watch. And then I will unleash you on him while I choose our toys of destruction."

She froze for a moment, letting out a low moan as I ran the backs of my fingers down her spine between her wings. They fluttered, the stained glass pieces reflecting the neon lights.

"Cinder," she whispered. "Witch."

"Your witch," I murmured, stepping closer.

My hand fell to her waist, and I held her still for a moment before lowering my lips to the back of her neck. She had worn her silver hair up in a bun today with a black spider and pearl clip.

I kissed her skin, breathing in her scent. Basking in her aura, in the lust that was radiating from the two of them. Mich and Lora both pulsed like neon lights, their auras blending together with mine to create a connection.

This was my favorite part about my abilities. To be able

to see how well we worked together. To feed off the magic we created just because our souls were meant to fit together.

My gaze locked with Mich's as I kissed our mate, touching her the way he wanted to touch her. His cock was standing straight up, precum glistening on the tip.

"Look at your toy, pet," I whispered. "Do you see it? Do you see his knot and spurs? Are you going to use it?"

"Yes," she whispered. "I'm going to use it while I mate."

"Yes, you are," I said, kissing her neck again. She shivered, her breath hitching. "I can't wait for us to mate him."

"We should at the same time."

"Yes," Mich moaned, pulling against his ropes. "Please. Please"

"Oh, he's already begging," I chuckled. "I can see the crazed heat overcoming him. The need to be fucked and mated. He's so desperate to feel your pussy around him again. He wants to feel our teeth on his neck as we bite him, to feel the magic of the spell I will speak."

"He's so desperate," Lora moaned.

"Desperate indeed. Just like you are," I said. "Strip, pet. Show us your body."

"Yes, witch."

I fought off a smile again. She was so sassy.

Lora took a step forward, looking down at Mich. He tore his pleading gaze from me and met hers, a low needy growl leaving him.

"Please," he moaned.

Lora began to strip, her clothes falling to the floor. Her pale skin turned blue and pink, her nipples and wings highlighted. I reached up and ran my fingers through her short silver hair, enjoying the way the locks caught the light.

I leaned down and ran my fingertips over the ridges

where her wings met her shoulders. She shuddered, a moan leaving her.

"Oh god," she gasped.

"You said no gods here," I murmured, drawing back. "Go play, pet. I'll join you soon."

Lora nodded and moved forward, crawling onto the bed and straddling Mich. I smiled as she sat on his chest, raking her claws down him.

Mich groaned, his body straining against the ropes. His tail and wings were spread out behind him, his claws curling into fists as she leaned down and swirled her tongue over one of his nipples.

Our manticore was done for.

With that, I turned and started to rummage through Lora's drawer of wonderful things.

CHAPTER FIFTEEN

## *mates*

MICH

My cock pulsed and my blood rushed in my ears. I took in a shallow breath before losing it to a gasp, the ropes keeping me in place as I tried to move.

I was helpless. Stuck with my demon and my witch, all of the worries from this week cast to the side. Everything that had happened didn't matter right now because fuck. FUCK.

Lora sucked on one of my nipples and I groaned, a beg slipping past my lips. "Please. Please."

"Please what?" Lora asked, smiling down at me.

Half of her face was drenched in shadow while the other half was caressed neon pink, her fangs glistening. She truly was a little monster, a beautiful one too. Everything about her was perfect, from the tip of her claws to her black eyes and silver wings.

"Please fuck me. Please mate me," I whispered. "Fuck. I've wanted you for so long. I want everything about you."

"I like it when you beg," she whispered. "Just like you liked hearing all the sounds I made while Cinder was marking me."

If my cock could have gotten any harder, it did. My eyes fell down to her chest, to the pink marks from the staples.

MINE.

She had left unhealed on purpose.

"I did," I admitted. "I liked hearing you cry. I liked feeling you clench around my tongue and cum as I gave you pleasure and they gave you pain."

"And now it's my turn," she said, grinning.

She rocked herself back and forth over me, pinching one of my nipples. I let out a hiss, my head falling back on her pillows.

"Oh. This is interesting."

I raised my head, looking over at Cinder for a moment. They were still rummaging through Lora's dresser, letting out evil giggles here and there.

Lora leaned down and I met her kiss, giving into her completely. If I was going to play the part of sacrifice, then so be it. I'd give them both everything.

She slid off of my chest to my side, still kissing me as she wrapped her hand around my cock. I groaned as our tongues fought, shivering with need as she began to stroke it up and down.

Her touch alone was nearly enough to send me over the edge. I couldn't think of anything else that had ever felt this good.

Cinder came back to us, standing at the foot of the bed. Their cuffs were rolled up their forearms, their shirt unbuttoned. The top button of their pants were undone too, giving me just a hint of the lace. Their hair was messed up now instead of slicked back like it was sometimes for work, their violet irises burning like stars.

Fuck. They were gorgeous.

They smiled, holding up something that made me damn near choke. Lora looked up and grinned.

"Yes," she said gleefully.

"Why do you have that?" I asked, my heart rate picking up.

It was a cock cage, one that looked like it might be big enough to contain me.

"This is for work tomorrow," Cinder said. "For you, dear monster. I just wanted to show it to you so you know what you will be doing in the morning."

"Yes, Master," I moaned.

Lora giggled and started to stroke me harder. "So submissive."

"He is," Cinder agreed. "A very good boy. He likes to please us."

I bit back a curse as she leaned down and flicked the tip of her tongue over the head of my cock.

"Lora," I moaned. "You're going to drive me crazy."

"Good," she said. "I like it when you're crazy, Mich. Especially when your cock is in my mouth."

I let out a low growl, my hips bucking up.

"Ride him," Cinder said.

"Sit on my face," I said, looking at them.

Cinder arched a brow. "Oh? Is that what you want?"

"Yes," I rasped. "I want her riding my cock while you ride my face. Please. Also I really like how you look right now."

"Oh yeah?" Cinder asked, stripping off their shirt.

"Yes," I said, fighting off a desperate moan. "Sexy."

Lora paused and looked up at them, smiling. "Our sexy witch."

Cinder smirked and let their pants fall to the ground.

"I love it when you wear lace," I groaned. "Fuck."

"Maybe after I ride you, I will fuck you," Cinder said.

"Please," I groaned.

Lora let out a low growl, her head tipping back for a moment. "Fuck. I need to taste you both."

"We'll bite you at the same time," Cinder said. "And then we'll fuck you at the same time."

"Yes," I whispered.

Fuck. I had known from the first moment I had seen both of them at the same time that I was theirs. That they were mine. Monsters always knew, always could sense when their mates were close by.

My rut had been caused because of these two and now it would end with them. And then I would spend the rest of my life loving them.

My chest thrummed with my heart beat, the feeling of desire and acceptance spreading through me.

Cinder came around to the other side of the bed and crawled on next to me, leaning down to kiss me. I took it, my head swirling with how lucky I was to have two mates. A witch and a demon, both charming and smart and sexy as sin.

Both of them willing to tie me up and fuck me too.

Cinder ran their fingers through my mane and then leaned down, offering me their neck.

Fuck. This was a moment I had been dreaming about my entire life. To be able to do a mating bite, to have someone that would always be with me...

Tears filled my eyes and I started with a kiss, listening to their little moan. Lora kept stroking my cock, pausing to watch as I finally sank my fangs into Cinder's neck.

Their breath hitched, their grip on me tightening as their blood filled my mouth.

I felt the bonds snap to life and growl, drinking more from them. Their blood was glorious, the taste of their magic crackling in my mouth. I drew back with a gasp, only to turn and see Lora smiling.

For a moment, all of the carnal lust that had been driving us crazy melted into something sweeter. Into something that I would never forget.

Her eyes softened as she swept her hair back and leaned forward, offering herself to me as well. I strained against my bonds as I lifted my mouth to her skin, piercing her with my fangs too.

A long groan left her, the taste of her blood filling my mouth now. It was completely different from Cinder's, and I felt myself groaning at how perfect both of them were for me.

Cinder's blood was sweet, Lora's was a little salty— and they were both perfect.

I drew back with a gasp. I could feel the connection strengthening with each moment that passed, and now it just had to be sealed by the two of them.

"I don't think my teeth will pierce you," Cinder whispered. "But I will speak the sacred spell. The one I never believed I would be able to, my love."

Heat spread through me and I realized a tear was rolling down my cheek. Cinder leaned forward and kissed it away, kneeling their forehead to mine.

Lora let out a little noise, moving in closer. She kissed down my chest, up to my neck. She breathed in my scent, releasing a breath.

"I'm ready," she whispered.

"Me too," Cinder said.

"Me too," I also said.

I could feel the swell of the moment. It was the type that even ages for now I would never forget. The lust, the tenderness, the fact that the three of us had finally found arms that would embrace us each.

Our love was new but it would burn forever. Our mated bond would tie our souls to each other until the end, and then beyond that.

I felt the rush of magic as the sacred spell left Cinder's lips, just as Lora's teeth pierced me. I let out a sharp cry, but it wasn't one of pain. It was of pleasure. It was of knowing that this was it— something that the three of us never believed we would find.

Love.

Family.

Cinder and Lora held onto me, both of them letting out a gasp as the mated bonds took root.

I could feel them both now, and they could feel me. The echo of their thoughts, of their feelings.

I could feel how lonely Cinder had been.

I could feel how scared Lora had felt.

And I knew that both of them could feel the yearning to be loved that had haunted me for ages now.

"Oh," Cinder whispered.

I opened my eyes, looking at both of them. Their faces shined with tears and a quiet sob escaped Lora.

"Fuck. I never believed I deserved this," she whispered.

Cinder pulled her close, the two of them holding onto me.

"Me neither," I whispered. "I'm thankful for both of you. I'm thankful for everything."

"It's a funny feeling," Cinder whispered. "To be able to feel how much both of you care. I've never had this."

"None of us have," Lora said, resting her head on my chest.

Cinder nodded, running their fingers through her hair. They looked down at me with a soft smile, and then leaned down to kiss me again.

Every touch was tender. Every kiss full of love.

For a few minutes, the three of stayed bound in each others arms.

Lora lifted her head after awhile, that wicked look twisting her expression.

Cinder and I both raised our brows, because we could feel it.

"I still want to fuck you."

I fought off a laugh, grinning. "I did agree to be tied down. It would be a shame if that didn't happen."

"And I did say we would ride you together," Cinder said, smiling.

"Well," I said. "I'm at your service. Mates."

# fangs and spurs

## LORA

My head was spinning with all of the emotions I could feel from my mates. Even Cinder, although we hadn't sealed our bond completely yet.

Cinder dragged me into a hungry kiss, the lust shared between all of us rekindling. My pussy throbbed, aching to be touched. To be filled.

Mich moaned as Cinder shoved me back. I straddled Mich's thighs and grabbed his cock, stroking it again.

It had never stopped being hard, the spurs still begging to be inside of me.

Cinder gripped Mich's head, forcing him to look at them. "Beg her to take your monster cock."

"Please," he said.

"Oh, you can do better than that," Cinder whispered. "Much, much better. Try again, slave."

"Please fuck me," Mich groaned. "Please use me like

you would your toy. I'm yours, your toy to please you. To do whatever you want."

"You are her toy," Cinder said. "And mine."

"Yes," Mich rasped.

I rose up and hovered over his cock, bringing the head to my entrance. I slowly began to lower myself, gasping with delight as he stretched me. Cinder watched, their eyes glowing with a hint of pride.

"Good girl," they said. "Look at how well you use your toy."

Fuck.

"And you're still marked as mine. A freshly mated little demon, desperate to be filled with his cum."

"Yes," I groaned.

It had been fun taking control, but now I wanted to give in to my desires. I wanted to let myself cave to the hunger, to the lust that was driving me crazy.

I gasped as his spurs rubbed against me, moaning as I took every inch.

"So big," I gasped.

"You can take him," Cinder said.

I nodded, tears blurring my vision for a moment as a wave of pleasure washed over me.

Cinder let out a groan and then turned over onto their knees, pulling off their lace thong. I watched through half-closed eyes, enjoying Mich's reaction as Cinder leaned down and kissed him again.

They were perfect. My mates.

I seated myself fully on Mich, the two of us growling together. This time it was different, our first time being mated while fucking. I could feel how much pleasure I brought him and knew he could feel what he did to me too.

I was so fucking wet and needy. It felt good to be filled

as much as possible, my pussy spread around his monster cock.

Cinder straddled Mich's chest and shoulders and leaned over him, planting their hands against my headboard.

"Fuck, Cinder," I groaned. "Your ass is perfect."

Cinder turned their head over their shoulder to look at me, giving me a wild grin before looking back down at Mich.

"Take it," they growled.

"Yes, Master," Mich gasped.

The sound of Mich sucking filled the room, and that made me even more wet. I gasped and lifted myself, planting my hands on his chest as I began to move back and forth.

"Oh fuck," Cinder and I both groaned at the same time.

I felt all of my tension melt, and I finally gave way to pleasure. I began to use his cock, fucking myself. I moved up and down, listening to the sounds of his groans and growls as he pleasured our Master.

And fuck. Cinder really did have a perfect ass, it wasn't fair.

Cinder's muscles rippled as they fucked Mich's mouth, their head tipping back with pleasure. I moaned in response, sliding my hand to my clit and rubbing as I rode him.

"Ah," I moaned. "Fuck. I'm getting close."

"Me too," Cinder groaned.

Mich let out a growl but wasn't able to form words, his mouth still busy and his limbs bound to my bed.

I bounced up and down on his cock, my head tipping back and my wings fluttering.

"Cum," Cinder growled. "Cum with me."

I gasped as I rode Mich harder, the edge so close. So fucking close.

Mich groaned loudly, and I knew he was about to cum, his body trembling beneath me. I moved faster, his cock thrusting in and out of me.

"Cum," Cinder snarled.

Cinder's demand was enough to send us over the edge.

Mich's knot filled me, locking inside of me just as his hot cum started to fill me. I cried out as I came, gasping as my orgasm wrecked through me. Wave after wave of pleasure overcame me, and I realized I was feeling the echoes from Cinder.

Echoes from Mich.

I groaned, small quakes working through me. Mich's knot sealed his cum inside of me, his chest heaving.

Cinder moaned and slid back, rolling to the side. With the flick of their hand, all of the ropes untied, and Mich grunted.

The three of us lay there together for a while, basking in the sound of our heart beating. I closed my eyes, drifting off until I felt Mich's knot start to slip free.

I slowly pulled off Mich with a groan, his cum immediately leaking out.

"How the fuck are you still hard?" I panted.

Mich chuckled and swept me into a hug, his burly arms wrapping around me. "I can't help it. When a rut happens, you know how it is."

I nodded and then rolled to the side. Cinder was on the other, the three of us breathing heavily.

All of us were in the clouds, floating in our own thoughts. Cinder's arm wrapped around Mich, his hand settling on me. I smiled, thinking about how crazy everything had become.

Cinder lifted their head, and I did too.

"I want to mate with you," they whispered.

"Yes," Mich whispered, grinning like an idiot. "Complete the circle."

"Shush," I giggled, pinching him. But I was grinning too. "I want to mate with you too, Cinder."

They smiled, and I sat up.

"Hold on," Mich said, holding up his hands. "I want to watch."

"And you will," Cinder chuckled, sitting up too.

We both leaned over, meeting in the middle over our mate to kiss. Cinder gripped the back of my head, drinking me in.

I kissed down their face, down their neck to where their pulse was. I let out a dark growl, my lips buzzing.

I could still taste Mich too.

"I will speak the spell," Cinder whispered.

I nodded, kissing them.

Then, I sank my teeth straight into their skin.

They whispered the spell as their blood filled my mouth, and we all made a noise as the bonds finally completed. I held on to them, drinking from them as I felt every piece of the puzzle fall into place.

Mich and Cinder were mine, and I was theirs.

I pulled back with a gasp, watching as the bite mark healed quickly from my saliva. It still left a faint silver scar, one that I would like to see flashing every now and then.

Cinder kissed me again, and then we both sank down.

Mich held us tight, the three of us holding on to this newfound love.

"I moved out here," I whispered, drawing their attention. "I moved out here to escape my ex. To get away from everything with him. And he made me believe that I would never find love like this. But now I have...."

Tears filled my eyes, and Mich held me a little tighter, Cinder's hand finding me again.

"And I didn't know it would be like this. I didn't know it would be so sudden and chaotic. But I'm glad it is. I'm glad to have you both now."

"I'm glad too," Cinder murmured.

Mich kissed the top of my head and let out a happy sigh. "I'm glad too."

"You're wearing that cock cage tomorrow," Cinder chuckled.

That made Mich groan, and me laugh.

Life was going to be a lot more fun with these two.

# hazard pay

## CINDER

I walked into Inferna's office, my heart pounding as I shut the door behind me. Art was sitting in the chair across from her, and he raised his hand, casting a spell so we would have privacy.

"Is she safe?" I asked.

"Yes," Inferna said. "She was scared and worried since she hasn't heard from you much this week."

I nodded, a pang of guilt working through me.

I had barely spoken to Ember this week. Between everything going on and the decision to have her taken somewhere no one could find her, we hadn't spoken.

It worried me, but I knew she was okay.

Plus, I knew she would hate that I worried so much. She didn't like to hide. In fact, she didn't like to be forced into doing anything.

That pang of guilt ran through me once again, stronger this time.

But then, it was answered with a wave of comfort from my mates. Both of them had come to work this morning with me, the three of us ready for battle.

Waking up next to them this morning had been a reminder that there was a future that didn't involve having to worry about this evil company. There was a way for me to have my mates while keeping Ember safe.

There was a way for me to be happy.

I still made Mich wear his cock cage, though.

"But she's safe," Infera said, sighing.

She looked tired, which felt out of character for her. I had only known her for a few days, but seeing her hold on to her cup of coffee like it was a lifeline made me feel uneasy.

"Are you both okay?" I asked, looking at Art too.

Art winced a little and then nodded. "Late night. Inferna was on the phone with extended family for a while, and then Calen had a nightmare about omega witches. I'm glad that you kept your sister safe. The things these people are doing are barbaric."

"They are," I said, fighting back the guilt.

I had a hand in some of the witches' fates. How did I make up for that?

I had done what I could, but knowing that other witches were hurting because of what I had helped them do...

*You have to forgive yourself*, Mich had told me last night.

How did I forgive myself?

"Cinder," Inferna said, arching a brow. "I can see the guilt eating you alive. You're going to have to let it go if we're going to make it to the weekend. Now that Ember has been taken, we've set things in motion. And also, maybe once things calm down again, she can work here too. I heard that she's a go-getter."

"She is," I whispered, taking the chair next to Art. "This has all become so complicated, but I am grateful for the help. Thank you for taking her somewhere safe."

Inferna nodded, taking a sip from her mug. "Alex is out of the office today too. He said he had 'unfinished business' in a very ominous tone before leaving like a little storm cloud."

I snorted, thinking about him.

He was an odd character, one that I wanted to distrust but couldn't find a reason to. His words were genuine, and for an ancient witch— he was honest enough.

Honest enough but not completely truthful. There was more going on, and I wondered how long it would take for our group to figure it out. Would more people have to get hurt?

"We know we can trust him, but we have chosen not to share any information with him," Art said. "None of us can fully grasp the extent of this power corruption, and he's already been in the crossfire once."

"True," Inferna said, smiling a little. "Just be aware today. If anyone starts acting strange, don't ignore it. And if you need help, just call. That goes for you and your mates."

"Thank you," I said.

Art and Inferna both nodded and then looked at each other.

I knew that look. One of love, of passion, of caring.

I had that now too. Not long ago, seeing two people look at each other that way would have made me look away. But now, it made me smile.

"Alright," I said, standing up. "I will let you know if anything comes up. Let me know if you need anything."

Inferna and Art both nodded. I left the two of them,

closing the door behind me. I went to the elevator, tapping the button to go down to our floor.

This week had felt like a whirlwind, and I was nervous. What now? What did I do now that Ember was safe?

I trusted Inferna when she said that no one would get to my sister. Whatever monsters she had connections to were fierce and protective.

The elevator was taking its sweet time. I let out a breath and hit it again but to no luck.

I glanced down the hall to the door where the staircase was.

It would take me less than a minute to take the stairs.

I looked back at the elevator and then rolled my eyes. Fucking elevators. I walked down the hall, opening the door and stepping into the stairwell.

I paused for a moment, a chill working up my spine.

Fuck.

I turned just in time to dodge the fist swinging for me. A dark figure slammed into me, knocking me into the wall.

I shoved them back, my heart pounding.

"Hazard," I snarled.

Shit. This wasn't good.

Hazard pinned me to the wall, his eyes burning with rage. He had the look of a witch ready to kill, the darkness rolling off him in waves.

"You fucking idiot," he growled. "Sleeping with the enemy? Mating with the enemy? Did you forget who owns you?"

I shoved him back, drawing up my magic to offer me a bit more protection— even though Hazard was ruthless.

"Not anymore," I growled. "I'm not doing this anymore. I'm done."

"You'll never be done," Hazard laughed. "Just like I will never be done. What about your sister?"

"You'll never find her," I said.

The two of us were squared off now, the lights flickering as the rage between us amplified.

"Just let me go, Hazard," I growled.

Hazard laughed again, his head tipping back. "You really think it's that simple? You're one of his favorites, Cinder. Always have been. You've always been given the easy jobs, the ones where all you have to do is manipulate people. And I bet that's what you did here too. To Lora and Mich. How does that stupid manticore act in bed? Submissive and breedable?"

"Don't even say their fucking names," I snarled.

Our magic was escalating more and more, the air becoming electric.

"Why? What are you going to do, Cinder? You may be trained in combat, but you're not a fucking fighter," Hazard said, smiling. "You don't stand a chance."

I lunged for him, only for the lights to burst above us. Glass rained down, and Hazard met me with full force, his angry red aura burning like a fire.

He kicked me in the gut, and I gasped, pain bursting through me as he grabbed me and shoved. I hit the edge of the stairs, rolling down the flight. Each bump rattled me, pain flaring over and over again until I hit the bottom.

My head swam in the dark, and I moaned, trying to force myself to get up.

I peeled my eyes open, looking up as Hazard stepped down the stairs slowly. Like a predator toying with its prey.

I pulled on my bonds, feeling the panic from Lora and Mich.

*In the stairwell.*

"Trying to call on them," Hazard chuckled, the sound of his boots making me flinch.

I sat up, pain burning through my ribs and left shoulder.

"I have them a little preoccupied," Hazard said, kneeling in front of me. "A little business meeting, if you will."

"If you hurt them," I growled. "I will burn you alive."

"You could try."

"What the fuck is happening here?"

Hazard and I both froze, turning to see one of the monsters from the office. One that I had yet to speak to this week. He was massive and had six eyes. His upper half was drenched in shadows, and I realized that he looked different in the dark.

In the office, he looked like a typical demon. But down here...

"Bilè. Leave," Hazard snarled.

"People call me Billy now. But I doubt you remember that, Hazard. I don't know what happened, but you need to take a step back, *traitor*."

"Billy," Hazard said, rising. "I will hurt you. Just like I've already hurt Cinder."

Two of Billy's eyes moved, looking at me.

I focused through the pain. Hazard was distracted enough in the moment for me to throw him off.

I took in a painful breath and slowly stood. Then, I lunged forward, running straight into him. Hazard hit the guardrail hard, the sound of bones cracking echoing around us.

Hazard screamed, his magic bursting from him. I was thrown back, but caught by Billy.

"Thanks," I gasped.

Billy nodded. "I swear to Satan they owe me workers comp at this point."

"I agree," I wheezed.

Hazard turned, letting out a fierce howl. "You will pay for that."

"Hazard pay," Billy mumbled.

That made me laugh despite the circumstances.

Hazard moved for us, and I threw up my arms, only to realize my mistake.

A portal cropped up behind the two of us, and Hazard shoved us both back, sending us straight through into the dark.

# fight and flight

## MICH

I HAD BEEN TRYING TO FIGURE OUT HOW I WAS GOING to take a piss with a cock cage on when a monster came into the bathroom, one I had never seen before.

I zipped up my fly and turned right as the bastard punched me, sending me straight into the wall.

"FUCK!" I yelled, looking up in confusion.

The lights flickered, and I felt pain run through me, but it wasn't mine.

Oh shit.

The monster who had just punched me into the wall was an orc, one that was bigger than any other I had ever run into.

"Listen," I said. "That was a solid punch. An eight out of ten. Four star rating. But you're fucking with a manticore. And I really don't feel like killing someone before noon this Thursday."

"I've been sent to kill you," the orc said, shrugging. "Fight to the death then. I don't care."

I stared at him, scoffing. "No sense of self-preservation?!"

"Not when they're watching," the orc said.

For a moment, just a moment— that made me wonder if the orc was being forced to do this.

But then he lunged at me full force, running straight towards me.

"Fucking hell," I cursed, dodging out of the way just in time.

The orc slammed into the wall, and I turned, raking my claws across his chest. He was wearing a polka-dotted button-down, and it shredded, his blood welling.

He was an orc, and orcs were fierce. But while I worked in the office now, I was still a manticore.

I was still going to end him if he didn't stop.

"Orc," I said again. "Please be reasonable. You're fighting a manticore."

This only made the green bastard angry. He let out a vicious roar, running towards me again. My tail darted around, the sharp tip slamming into his ribs.

His knees buckled immediately, the venom shooting into him.

I let out another sigh, stretching my jaw. "Sorry," I said, yanking the scorpion tip free. "I really hate using that. You're going to sleep now."

The orc's eyes were already fluttering. He slumped back, hitting the cold floor.

Fuck.

I felt another flash of pain from my bond with Cinder, the panic radiating.

*In the stairwell.*

Fuck.

I stole another look at the orc and then turned, rushing out and into the office. A few coworkers looked up at me, and I let out a roar. "Someone get the boss!"

One of my coworkers stood up, but then their expression darkened.

Oh, fuck no.

"Mich!"

I looked up to see Lora running towards me, blood splattered across her blouse and dripping from her nails.

Another coworker stood up, one that was a witch.

The others started to move, sensing a fight. Everyone was frozen, their eyes darting between us and the two who had just stood.

"I just put your orc friend in a coma," I growled. "And he's bleeding in the bathroom. You really want to fight?"

"We have to," the witch growled.

"What's your name?" I asked.

I fought the urge to look to my left as I heard a soft hiss. I could see Anne creeping up behind them out of the corner of my eye, ready to pounce.

Lora was ready too, a low growl leaving her.

"Do you really want to die here today?"

"I don't think they have a choice," I said. "So maybe if they pretended to fight us and we knocked them out real nice, they could live to see another Thursday."

The two of them glanced at each other, and then the witch shook his head.

"No. Our orders are to fight you until your mate is gone. And we've almost done that."

Fuck it.

Some of the monsters and witches let out squeals, their eyes wide as I jumped forward. Anne made the strike faster though, moving behind the two of them with lightning speed. My mouth dropped open in shock as they were knocked out within seconds, both slumping to the floor.

"Anne!" Lora said. "Oh, thank god."

Anne let out a hiss. "I'm so sick of this shit."

"Same," I said, already moving towards the front of the office.

Lora caught up to me, and then we both started running.

"Where the fuck is Calen?" Lora asked.

"I don't know," I growled, throwing open the stairway door.

The two of us hit the flight just in time to see none other than fucking Hazard disappearing through a portal.

"No," Lora whispered.

My knees felt weak, my stomach dropping. I could feel the panic through my bonds to Cinder and Lora. The terror, the pain, and then...

It stopped.

Lora let out a choked cry. "What does that mean?!"

"I don't know," I whispered. "I don't know. It'll be okay. We need to find the others."

"We have to go after them now!"

"Lora," I growled, turning to look at her.

Both of us were covered in blood and on edge. I was ready to tear open every enemy that tried to hurt us, my muscles burning with energy.

"Mich! Lora!"

That was Anne's voice. We both went back into the hallway just as the elevator doors opened. Inferna, Art, and Calen all stepped out— covered in blood just like we were.

"I'm about to murder everyone! " Inferna yelled. "What the fuck is wrong with these bastards?!"

"Hazard took Cinder," Lora said.

Our group met in the center, Anne included. We could all hear the yelps and squeals coming from the main office, everyone scared.

"Are the three of you okay?" I asked.

"Yes," Art said, his arm around Calen. "A monster and witch attacked us in the office, but we handled them. For fuck's sake, we need to call Alex."

"No," Inferna said. "No. Whatever he was doing, it was important. We can handle this. Are you okay? And Anne, you too?"

"I'm fine," Anne said, shaking her head. She let out a hiss, her diamond eyes filled with rage. "I want a raise."

"We'll bully Alex into it," Art said, glaring. "I want one too at this point."

"I bet they took them to wherever their boss is," Calen said. "Didn't Cinder say they were across the street? It's probably close by like it was last time."

Fear worked through me, and I looked over at Lora, slipping my hand into hers. Both of us were scared of losing them, scared that Cinder would be hurt.

"Also, Billy is missing," Anne said. "And he usually takes the stairs. I wonder if he was taken."

"Or if he's part of it," Inferna said. "Either way, we will find out. What's the company that works across the street?"

"It's a security company," Anne answered. "They actually run the security in the lobby."

All of us were silent for a moment as the information settled over us.

Fuck, we really were surrounded.

"I might put in my two weeks after this," I muttered.

"I wouldn't blame you if you did," Inferna said.

"Although I really just want to burn it down from the inside."

I smiled a little. Her fierceness was inspiring enough to distract me from the fear and numbness taking over.

"I'm going to punch that fucker if I see him," I growled. "Hazard. Fucking bastard."

"Get in line," Lora growled, squeezing my hand.

"I might be able to use your mating marks to track Cinder," Art said, looking between the two of us. "How do you feel about a ritual?"

"Whatever needs to be done to get Cinder back is good enough for me," Lora said.

I nodded, all of us agreeing.

"Alright," Art breathed, looking down at Calen. "Four monsters, two witches. I think we've got this."

# *rituals*

LORA

The six of us crowded into the stairwell where the portal had disappeared, Art standing in the center. He glowed a soft blue hue, sparks of magic coming from his fingertips as he raised his hands.

Mich and I held out our hands, palms up.

I was scared, not scared of Art or this ritual, but that it wouldn't work and that we would lose Cinder.

We'd finally all found each other. Finally found a shred of happiness in this world. And then this happened.

I was desperately trying not to let my own darkness consume me, but it was hard. None of this was fair to any of us.

That, and I couldn't feel Cinder like I had been all morning and night.

I closed my eyes, trying to fight back the tears. I felt Anne's hand settle on my shoulder gently, offering me comfort.

"It'll be okay," Anne whispered. "Cinder will be okay."

I nodded, taking a deep breath.

Inferna and Calen were both watching Art intently, concerned.

"There might be another way to track them, Art," Inferna said, her voice soft. "I know you hate blood magic."

"I do," Art said, wincing. "But it's the only way. It worked last time, so why not this time?"

Inferna looked like she wanted to argue but didn't say anything, giving him a slight nod.

"This might hurt," Art warned, looking up at us. "And I don't know how effective it will be since I'm not connected to either of you. But we can try."

"Whatever we can try," Mich whispered.

"I hope it works," I said. "I don't know how else..."

"We will find a way, Lora," Anne said.

I gave her a weak smile. I was glad she was here, thankful to know that she wasn't like the witches and monsters that had attacked us.

I had been trying to get a cup of coffee when I'd been cornered. It hadn't gone well for them, and I hated every moment of that fight.

"I'm sorry for the pain," Art said.

It could be the worst pain in the world, and it wouldn't matter so long as we could find Cinder.

Art ran the tip of his finger over our palms, slicing our skin open as if his touch were that of a sharp blade. I held back a small hiss as the blood started to well. Art gripped both of our hands with his, closing his eyes.

I was a demon, but I still didn't understand the words he spoke. We felt the rush of magic in the stairwell, everything was covered in bright blue as our witchy boss began to glow brighter. Pain began to radiate up my arm, consuming my body in a hot flash. I gasped as it grew hotter, the bite mark from Mich pulsing as if it were being zapped.

Art let out a frustrated noise, the glow dying. "It's not working," he said, looking back at Inferna.

"I think if you change the spell, it will work," Calen said.

"If I change it wrong, I could turn these two to ash," Art said.

All of us paled at the thought of that.

"Fuck," Mich sighed.

Anne crossed her arms, visibly thinking. Her snakes were drawn back in a bun, her glasses pushed up her nose. She hummed. "I have an idea. Well, maybe."

"What?" Mich asked.

"Well, Lora is a demon, and so is Billy. If I remember correctly, demons are able to summon each other. Right? For other creatures, you have to know the words. But for demons... well, unless that's a myth."

It wasn't a myth, but it wasn't exactly true either. Some demons could, but I had never tried to summon another.

All eyes turned to me, and I let out a breath. "I don't know. Some demons are able to but I've never summoned another before. I can try, but I don't know exactly how."

"If you focus on something of theirs then you should be able to," Anne said. "Oh! I will be back. I can get something from his desk."

"Okay," I said.

Anne was already moving, disappearing out into the office.

I held my palm to my lips and licked it, watching the cut heal.

"Well, that was...unexpected," Art said, grinning. "Didn't know you could do that."

"Well," I said, smiling. "I'm not just a demon. I'm part fae as well. Makes for some interesting abilities."

"I can imagine," Inferna chuckled.

I grabbed Mich's hand and kissed his palm, watching as it healed. Mich tugged me close for a moment, kissing the top of my head.

"We'll find them."

I buried my face in his chest, breathing in his scent.

Last night had been magical, and today was hell.

The door to the stairwell opened and closed, Anne appearing with a water bottle.

"Here you go," she said. "His desk is weirdly neat."

I snorted, knowing that even though Anne kept everyone organized, her own desk was often a mess.

I took it from her, holding it in front of me. I closed my eyes, not sure what I was doing. What the hell was I doing?!

I needed Cinder. I had to find them and save them.

We knew that something could happen once Ember was taken, but we didn't expect it to be so soon. We also hadn't expected them to show up and fucking kidnap Cinder.

But....I knew they were in trouble. They had already been scared of what could happen, knowing that even touching Mich or me could bring trouble.

I didn't regret a goddamn thing...but I needed them back.

I took a deep breath, steadying myself. I was a demon, a powerful one. I chose to work in an office environment but if it were the days of old, I would have been worshiped.

Maybe a little feared too.

I felt a surge of energy rush through me, and I focused on Billy, the six-eyed demon I'd been working with for a few months. We had never talked much, but he had always been nice. He was an older demon— much, much older despite the fact he looked young.

I could feel all of them around me, waiting to see what would happen.

I could feel the comfort coming from Mich, could hear the flutter of his heartbeat. I focused on it, letting the sound move through my entire body. I focused on the darkness, reaching into it. Into the shadows that haunted demons and fae alike.

In my mind, I drew a circle. The water bottle that belonged to Billy was an amplifier, a lifeline, a way to the demon that was with my mate.

They may have blocked Cinder from us, but they couldn't block this.

A low growl echoed around me, and the darkness began to pull into a form with six crimson eyes, antlers, and the legs of a satyr.

*Lora. You summoned me?*

*Where are you? Where is Cinder?* I asked.

*Fuck. We don't know. We're both in a room alone, but they can't use their magic. I also can't reach out, although it seems like you can reach in.*

*We're going to find you,* I said quickly. *Give me anything. Something that will help.*

*The portal dropped us into an office, but it was empty. All of the blinds were pulled down so we couldn't see outside. It's cold and quiet, and the only movement is from witches or creatures. Cinder is supposed to meet their boss and I think they will be harmed.*

*We're going to stop that from happening.*

*You can track me, Lora. Has a demon ever shown you how?* Billy asked, looking me over.

I shook my head. I've never been taught much about the demon side of my family, even though most of my strengths come from them.

*Whatever item you used to call on me, keep it with you. It will help guide you. Wherever we are, the portal was a quick and short one. It wouldn't have taken us far. It's not our building but....*

*Maybe the one across the street. Did you see any security clothing on anyone? Or anything like that?*

*I have to go,* Billy said. *Someone is about to walk in. But yes. Blue badges with a centaur holding a shield as the emblem.*

I opened my mouth to ask more, but Billy went up in smoke, and the circle disappeared.

My eyes flew open, and I gasped. I would have fallen to my knees, but Mich caught me, picking me up before I hit the ground.

"I got you," he huffed. "That was scary. Your eyes turned white for a moment."

I felt drained, but I pushed forward, looking around at our rag tag group of work culture rejects. "I saw him. Billy. He couldn't tell where they were exactly, but they're in an office. And there have been creatures wearing blue badges with a centaur and shield emblem."

"Damnit," Art growled. "That's the security company."

"Of course," Inferna sighed. "If it's not the HR company, of course it would be the security one. Why not both."

"At this point, why not?" Calen asked, shaking his head. "They're evil."

"They are," I agreed. "They're going to hurt Cinder. We have to go. Billy said I can track them with the water bottle."

"Good," Anne said. "I knew you could do it."

I smiled at her as Mich let me down, his hand still on me.

"Alright," Inferna said. "Plan. We need a plan. And I think I might just have one."

# horny resources

## CINDER

Billy and I stared at the door as it flew open. Part of me expected Hazard to walk in again, but instead, it was someone much, much worse.

Someone I had really hoped wasn't working today.

"Well," she said, arching a brow. "Unfortunate to see you on this side of the door, Cinder."

With a name like Parsley, one would think that the witch standing in front of us was just an innocent one. Not one that was known for being the boss's right-hand woman. An executioner when needed, someone who vehemently hated almost everyone.

Someone who had passive-aggressiveness down to a T.

She wore a black pencil skirt, heels, and a crimson red blouse that fought with her already bright red bob. She arched a perfectly drawn eyebrow, glaring at me.

"I haven't done anything wrong," I said.

"Liar," she said, smiling. "Such a liar. You've never been

good at it either, Cinder. Your sister is missing, and you've been fucking two of the office monsters every spare moment you get. I can see the fucking mated bonds. Have you lost your mind? Have you forgotten who owns you?"

"Not anymore," I growled. "I'm done. I quit."

"You don't quit this job, Cinder. You either retire or get fired. And when you get fired, it's straight down to the depths of hell where all of us belong."

"I would say none of you belong in hell since you're not demons," Billy chimed in.

We both looked at him. Hell, I'd almost forgotten he was in the room.

He was also tied up but not in bad shape like I was. My ribs and shoulder ached with radiating pain, and blood dripped from my forehead.

"Who the fuck are you?"

"Billy," he said, his six eyes regarding her with equal disdain. "Who are you?"

"Probably your death, demon," Parsley snapped.

"Fun. I mean, if you manage that, then props to you. What is all of this?"

She stared at him for a moment like he was an idiot and then shook her head. "Annoying. This is the HR department for your company, and also the security. We watch everything that happens in the office and listen to every single thing. We watch you come into work and leave."

"And yet you didn't know who I was," Billy chuckled. "So you're the bastards that made us merge with the other office so you can get the omegas. There aren't that many around, you know. And I can't imagine what you're doing with them."

She glared at him, her jaw stiffening. "It's none of your

business, monster. And sadly, we'll have to figure out how to end you now, thanks to your wonderful HR agent."

"Leave him alone," I grit out. "The only reason he's here is because Hazard fucked up. That's Hazard's punishment. Just make him sign an NDA, and he can go home."

"No," Parsley said simply. "We can't be so kind anymore. Not after everything that has happened. Alice and Claude murdered, parts of our plans exposed, and now a defective agent. Even though your sister is one of them."

"Fuck you," I said. "Fuck you. I don't care if you fucking kill me, Parsley. I fucking quit. I hope all of you are caught and face punishment for every terrible thing you've done."

"Don't act so innocent," she growled. "You've done the same damn things. And whatever your excuse is, it doesn't matter. You're just as damned as I am, Cinder. And now you have to explain yourself to him."

Fuck, I'd never actually spoken to him.

"He wants to pick your brain," she said, giving me a slimy smile. "To see what could lead one to do something so stupid after we've been so kind."

I glared at her, but she twisted her hand, and her magic forced me to my feet.

"Try not to resist so much," she chimed, opening the door. "It won't hurt as much then."

I was about to snap a bitter answer when the lights went out, the sound of the power dying. Parsley's magic cast a soft glow, but she growled, looking up.

"What just happened?"

A glimmer of hope moved through me, and she turned, shoving me back.

I hit the floor as the door slammed shut.

"I think that's our boss," Billy said. "Both of them."

"What was happening before she walked in?" I asked,

rolling to my side and sitting up. My arms were bound behind my back, but I was still able to move decently well.

"Your mate summoned me. Even though this room is suppressing us, she could reach in."

"Lora?" I asked, trying to fight back the bite of panic.

I didn't want them coming here. If Mich and Lora showed up and were trapped, there would be nothing I could do to protect them from anything. There was no telling what would happen.

"Yes. I'm sure it'll be okay. Plus, I have my ties undone now," Billy said, raising his hands.

"Oh fuck," I said, grinning.

He smiled and leaned forward. They had wrapped a chain around my wrists, but his talons were sharp enough that within a moment, they fell to the floor.

I pulled my hands forward, rubbing my wrists with a hiss. "Thank you. I'm sorry I never said hi before."

"You were busy," Billy said, shrugging. "I just work here, witch."

I let out a sigh of relief as he stood. He reached down, helping me stand.

"You have some broken bones," he said. "I can feel them. Just lean on me, and we'll get out."

"How are you so unconcerned?" I asked.

"I'm about 789 years old," he said. "Ain't my first rodeo. And these walls are a lot thinner than the ones they made years ago."

He helped me walk to the door, and I pulled it open. We both leaned forward, hearing muffled shouts and yelling.

I could feel my bonds again.

*Where are you?!* I heard Lora squeal.

*Billy and I are escaping, but I'm injured.*

"Tell her I will get us out," Billy said. "Now that we're out of that room, I'll take us through a portal."

*We're getting out.*

Billy helped me limp forward into the open space. I was about to ask a question when we both froze.

A chill ran up my spine, followed by fear.

"Cinder," a deep voice said. "Leaving so soon? We haven't had a chance for our one-on-one."

Billy helped me turn around to meet the gaze of a black werewolf with golden eyes. He was wearing a black suit with a navy tie, a silver watch gleaming in the dark.

This was him.

"You," I growled.

He smiled, his canines glinting. "Oh yes. Me. The big bad wolf. The reason your world is crumbling."

Anger flashed through me, and I pulled away from Billy, fighting to stand on my own. "It's nice to finally see you face to face."

"I'm sure," he said. "It's not over, little one. It won't be. This is my company. The things that we're doing can't be stopped. And even if your sister is safe, it doesn't matter. There are plenty of others out there. So do me a favor."

"As if I would ever do you a fucking favor," I snarled.

He cocked his head, and I fought off the shiver wracking me.

It truly felt like he was going to devour us.

Billy let out a low warning growl behind me, one for this evil bastard.

"Tell Alex that we're coming for him. Tell him that this is all his fault. And no matter what he does to try and stop it, he will not be able to. This company that we started so long ago is mine, not his. And last but not least..." he took a step forward, and I realized that he was leaning on a cane. He raised it, pointing it at me. "You're fired, Cinder. Remember that I showed you mercy when the office is torn to pieces."

"Come on," Billy growled.

I held his gaze for a moment longer and then turned. Billy raised his hands, drawing a circle in the dark. Before I could turn back to steal another look at the werewolf that had truly messed up my life, he threw me into it, following behind me.

The two of us landed in the middle of Alex's office, hitting the floor hard.

I groaned, pain flaring through my body again. I let out a grunt, rolling onto my back.

I stared at the ceiling tiles, realizing it was well past the office being closed. The last of the light threw rays of sunset over everything.

"That was eventful," Billy sighed, spread out on the floor next to me. "I think I will take the elevator next time. Fuck getting my steps in."

I smiled, lifting my head to look over at him. "Thanks. You didn't have to help me."

Billy shrugged. "Sometimes demons are good."

I heard the sound of footsteps and looked behind us.

"Cinder!"

Lora and Mich turned the corner, running straight for me.

I choked on a noise, trying to sit up to meet them, but I was immediately pulled into their arms. I hissed as pain flared through me again, and Lora let out a squeal.

"You're hurt! Oh gods," she rasped.

Mich grabbed my face, his eyes wide with worry. "Are you okay?"

"Aside from broken bones, yes," I said, pulling both of them tight to me.

Relief washed through me, and I could feel every emotion through our bonds. Love, worry, relief. The three of us held on to each other as if we were each other's lifelines.

Tears rolled down my cheeks, and I wiped them away, relaxing against them.

I wasn't sure I was going to see them again.

I heard more voices now and looked past them. Inferna, Art, Calen, and Anne were all here— talking to each other and Billy. I could barely focus on their words, so instead, I focused on my mates.

Lora reached up and grabbed my face, pulling me into a hungry kiss. I took it, savoring her taste. Savoring her touch.

My head started to swim as my pain began to numb. She pulled back but didn't let go of my face. "That should help until we get you home," she whispered. "Fuck. I thought we lost you, Cinder."

"I thought I lost both of you," I said, looking up at Mich.

He nodded, his arms still holding me tight. "I was scared. But Lora is amazing and was able to track Billy. And Inferna came up with a plan. And we were able to distract them long enough while Billy got you both out."

"We were let go," I said, my voice hoarse.

Knowing that didn't make anything better.

He had let us go.

He knew what he was doing.

"Cinder," Inferna said, drawing my attention. "We will all meet about this tomorrow. But I think we are all safe for tonight."

"We are," I said, thinking about the werewolf's words. "I was officially fired, but without the death sentence."

"Well," Art said. "For once, that sounds like a good thing."

We all nodded, and I winced. "Billy, thank you again."

Billy raised a shadowy hand. "Stop, witch. We were both in danger. But you're welcome. Can I go home now?"

"Yes," Inferna said, grinning. "Thanks for the overtime."

Billy snorted and then shook his head, leaving our group.

Anne let out a sigh. "I'm done for today too."

"Yes. Everyone go home, please," Inferna said.

"Us included," Calen said.

"Us too," Mich chuckled. "Thank you for everything."

Inferna shrugged but grinned. "That's what we're here for. Now, let's go home. Cinder, if any of you need anything, just call. I'm salaried, after all."

With that, Mich picked me up and carried me to the elevator.

At least tomorrow was Friday.

## CHAPTER TWENTY-ONE

# *friday*

MICH

THE THREE OF US HAD SPENT LAST NIGHT MAKING SURE Cinder was okay. We'd all cuddled in bed, had dinner, talked through what had happened, and then woke up this morning to come to work.

Hell, I didn't want to be here. I wanted to be back in bed with my mates. I wanted to make some French toast and drink coffee and talk about all of the knitting stuff Lora was into. Or learn more about Cinder's sister.

But, we needed to have the meeting.

We were lucky yesterday.

Cinder had been lucky.

I had never been so scared of losing someone, but Inferna's plan had worked.

"Alright," Alex said, standing up at the head of the meeting table.

All nine of us were crammed into an office. Cinder sat between Lora and me, with Anne to my left. Inferna, Art,

Calen, and Billy sat across from us, with Alex at the head of the table.

"Where were you yesterday?" Lora asked, glaring.

She wasn't happy with Alex being part of this meeting, but Cinder and Inferna had insisted it was important.

"I had to do something," Alex said. "I'm sorry I wasn't here to help. We all take days off every now and then."

"Really convenient," Lora muttered.

Infera arched a brow and leaned back, looking at our boss. Alex stood, unphased by Lora's snide comment and still wearing an easy going smile.

We all knew he wasn't easy going.

"Yesterday," Inferna said, clearing her throat. "Cinder and Billy were taken by Hazard, an ex-employee who disappeared the same week that Alice attacked us. Mich and Lora were then attacked by other employees and someone who had slipped in. They were knocked out. I fired them this morning, well, the one that came back anyway. The others have not shown back up. Anne helped Lora and Mich stop them, while Art, Calen, and I dealt with a monster and a witch who attacked us upstairs. We came down after, all met, and realized that Cinder had been taken, along with Billy. After that, Art and Calen used their magic to cut the power lines leading to the building across the street. The power went out, and our theories were proved correct. The person that is controlling all of this was housed across the street. Billy was able to draw up a portal to take Cinder out, and they escaped."

Inferna had omitted a couple of things, but none of us interjected.

"He stopped me before we left," Cinder said, looking directly at Alex. They sounded tired and a little angry, their body still sore even though they had already done quite a bit of healing. "He wanted me to tell you something. But before I do that, I think you should tell us how you know that werewolf bastard. The one that you apparently started this company with. And which company? The witch side? The monster side? Didn't this just merge together? You have some explaining to do."

Alex picked up his mug of coffee, taking a long sip. An uncomfortably long sip. He then exhaled and plopped down in his chair. "It's complicated."

"No," Art growled. "Don't give us that shit."

Alex arched his brow. "Language."

"No," Cinder said, leaning forward. "Fuck language. This was a life or death situation. You can't act like it was nothing. Why is this happening? Why are they taking omega witches? Why is this office targeted?"

Alex held up a hand. "Ask me another question, and I'll start to forget. First, tell me what he told you."

"Absolutely not," Inferna hissed. "Answer the questions, Alex."

His eyes darkened, the tension in the room increasing. I shifted in my chair, leaning forward to glare at him.

"Everyone calm down. I'm not the bad guy," Alex said. "But I did make some mistakes. The werewolf that you are referring to— his name is Alfred. He's a creature who has been around for a long time. The two of us started working together years ago, on different adventures. Never had any issues. We were good friends even. But then he changed, and by the time it was too late, we'd already started a large modern company together. I thought he had left the picture and that Claude had taken over his side, which was why I agreed to the merger."

Inferna leaned forward in her chair, her growl menacing. "This would have been great information before, Alex.

We've been working together for weeks, and you didn't feel like this was good info to know?"

"It didn't seem too relevant yet," Alex said, looking at her.

Inferna growled, but Art put his hand on her shoulder, giving her a gentle tug back.

"Go on," Art said, glaring.

"So we did the merger, and all hell broke loose," Alex sighed. "They captured me, and then the three of you went through your events. And then they sent us Cinder. And I knew they had, but my instincts were right about you."

"If you knew, why didn't you tell me?" Inferna hissed.

"Why didn't you or Art tell me?" Alex rebutted, giving her a thoughtful look as he took another sip of his coffee. "Sometimes, you have to see how things turn out."

"Not when people's lives are on the line!" Lora growled.

"No one died," Alex said. "Which is progress from our last encounter. And I'm not ending the company. We do good work for creatures. All kinds of creatures. The world is changing and having an app like ours makes a difference. It's getting harder and harder to hide. This thing with Alfred, we will stop him."

"He wasn't so convinced," Cinder said. "What are they doing with the omega witches?"

"Alfred has plans with them. I really don't know what," Alex said, scowling. "I do know this. I'm determined to stop him. I'm determined to end him. But, it takes time. It takes outsmarting him. What all of you did yesterday was intelligent and fast thinking. You were able to rescue Cinder, and Cinder was successfully fired without dying."

"And my sister is safe. But what about all of the other witches?" Cinder asked.

"Well, some of the ones who were rescued were

supposed to start this week, but I pushed it to next. So we will have a lot of training to do. And we will keep them safe. I have connections too, just like Inferna here."

"Yes," Inferna snapped. "But your connections aren't as good as mine."

"But they still are loyal," Alex said. "And they will make sure that the farther we go, the ones that escape will remain out of their hands. It will take them some time to recover after yesterday. And I imagine we will see a new tactic since our HR agent role is now filled permanently."

We all stared at him, and then I shook my head, leaning back in my seat and glancing around. All of us were pissed, but at least we were all safe. And at least we had more info now that Alex was being more transparent.

Cinder stood up, their gaze on Alex. "'Tell Alex that we're coming for him. Tell him that this is all his fault. And no matter what he does to try and stop it, he will not be able to. This company that we started so long ago is mine, not his.' That's what he told me to tell you," Cinder said.

Silence settled over the room. Alex frowned, the shadow returning to his gaze.

Our boss was shady at best, but at least he wasn't evil.

Well, from what we knew so far.

"Well then," Inferna said, looking from Cinder to Alex.

Cinder cleared their throat and then pushed the chair back. "So some of what you're saying makes sense, but you're hiding other things too. Regardless, I'm done for today, as are my mates. I am still healing after falling down a flight of stairs and dealing with a raging witch."

Lora started to stand, and I followed her, the three of us now out of our seats.

"We'll see everyone Monday," Cinder said.

Inferna nodded, standing up as well. "Thank you. I'm glad that you're safe, Cinder."

"Me too," I grumbled, looking over at them.

They nodded, giving her a genuine smile and then another brooding glare at Alex, who was silent.

I gave a little wave to Billy and Anne and then headed for the door. Lora and Cinder followed after.

The three of us made it through the office, to the elevator, and then to the garage within a few minutes. We all piled into my car, which was the only one that seemed to be able to fit the three of us well enough.

Cinder let out a long groan. "That was fucking torture."

"I don't like him," Lora grumbled, glaring.

I nodded, thinking about everything that he had said. "He's hiding stuff. But it doesn't matter now."

"No," Cinder chuckled, leaning back in their seat. "It's the weekend, and I'm free. I have two wonderful mates. And my sister is safe."

"And not only is it the weekend," I said, grinning as I pulled out onto the road. "We're out before noon. Half-day for the win."

"I think we deserve it after everything," Lora said, but she smiled too. "Cinder, how are you feeling?"

"Like I want to get home and fuck both of you."

"Well then," I stammered, feeling my cock already harden.

"I'm going to fuck Mich," Cinder said. "Especially since he wore a cock cage during a crisis yesterday."

It was true, I had done that.

"I think I can support this plan," I said, looking over at them.

Cinder smirked, looking back at Lora. "And then you, sweetheart. Maybe he can fuck you while I fuck him."

Lora let out a little moan. "That would be nice."

"Nice," Cinder snickered.

"Shut up," she laughed.

"It'll be nice."

I barked out a laugh. "Only ten minutes, and then we'll be at my place."

"Ten minutes until we all have a nice time."

# off the clock

## LORA

CINDER PUSHED ME DOWN ONTO MY KNEES NEXT TO Mich, their violet eyes burning with lust. We had rushed home, all eager to forget about this week.

Except for the good parts.

Monday, we realized there was something more to the three of us. Tuesday and Wednesday, we'd done some very naughty things off the clock. Thursday, all hell had broken loose, but now?

Now it was Friday, and we were done for the week.

We could forget about work, about all the troubles with the HR department. Forget about Alex and his cryptic words.

Cinder reached down, cupping each of our faces in their hands.

"Master," Mich whispered.

I shivered, allowing myself to submit. Allowing myself to completely give in.

"Are you sure you're okay?" I asked.

Cinder nodded. "I wouldn't have you on your knees if I weren't. Your concern is sweet, but I'm more than fine, thanks to you and Mich."

I nodded, releasing a pent up breath.

"You did so good," Cinder said softly, running their fingers through Mich's mane. "You obeyed me even in the middle of all the chaos. Such a good boy. And now you'll be rewarded."

I was already turned on just listening to them speak to Mich.

"I love you," Cinder said gently. They then looked at me, and my vision blurred with tears. "I love you too. Very much. I can't express how much both of you mean to me. This week has been a whirlwind. And it was hard. I've never been so scared and so happy in my life. But I wouldn't change a damn thing."

"I wouldn't change it either," I whispered.

Cinder leaned down, our lips meeting. The kiss was soft and gentle but with a sharp and aching edge. I groaned, accepting more. I rose up, my wings fluttering behind me in the same beat as my pussy.

They drew back and then leaned over to Mich, kissing him with the same passion. I watched my manticore mate melt under the touch, his muscles visibly relaxing.

Fuck.

"Master," I whispered.

"Yes, pet?" they asked.

"I want you."

Cinder smiled and gave Mich a small push. "On the bed, slave. Come here, pet."

Mich rose up immediatcly, moving over to the bed.

Mich and I had already stripped, our bodies naked and ready.

I wanted to be with them, to give them myself completely.

I went to Cinder, and they pulled me to standing, giving me a gentle push. "Get on the bed and lay your back on his chest. Little slave, I want you to keep her thighs parted for me."

"Yes, Master," we both said.

Anticipation ran through me. I wondered what they were going to do now.

"I'm going to do what I said," Cinder said. "I'm going to fuck Mich while he fucks you. But I want to see your face while he does, and I want to get you both warmed up first."

I was already wet, but I still obeyed them. I climbed up onto Mich's massive bed, and he smirked as I crawled on top of him. I paused for a moment to run my claws up his chest, pinching one of his nipples.

He grunted, his eyes fluttering for a moment.

I grinned, and he came to, glaring. "Rude," he chuckled.

"Just had to make sure they were working."

He snorted and flipped me over onto my back, my head falling on his shoulder. His hands gripped under my thighs, and he spread me open.

I looked down. I had the perfect view of Cinder and of Mich's hard cock. Cinder slowly undressed, their eyes on my pussy and Mich's cock.

I groaned. Their look alone made me wet, made me want more. There were so many things I wanted to do and try with them.

"Neither of you may move while I warm you up," Cinder said, hiding their smile as they pulled off the last piece of clothing. They came to the edge of the bed, crawling onto it. "Be still."

I already knew it was going to be a challenge.

Cinder leaned down, the tip of their tongue barely grazing over my clit. I gasped, and my legs would have moved, but Mich kept me in place with a groan.

"Fuck," he growled.

Cinder grinned, and then their eyes flicked up to us, watching as their tongue dipped inside of me.

I let out a squeal, and then Mich growled under me, followed by a moan. I looked down and realized that Cinder was now stroking Mich's cock while they licked me.

Warming us up.

Fuck.

"Master," I cried as they moved their mouth back up to my clit.

They nibbled it, sending shockwaves of pleasure through my entire body. My nipples hardened, heat rushing across my skin.

"Fuck," Mich groaned. "Fuck, you smell so good when you're turned on."

Mich did too. His scent was one that made me want to fuck until I couldn't anymore. I let out another gasp as Cinder continued, driving the two of us crazy.

"I'm going to cum," I panted, fighting my own muscles. "Master," I cried, "please don't stop. Please."

Mich's claws dug into my thighs. Cinder increased the pressure of their tongue, fucking me with it.

A cry tore through me, and I tried to move, but Mich kept me as still as possible as I came. Pleasure tore through me, an intense rush of euphoria following.

Cinder drew back with a satisfied smirk, licking their

lips. I was already floating on cloud nine when I heard more noises.

I groaned, my muscles fully relaxed. I looked down, watching as Cinder started to suck Mich's cock.

Mich gasped, and I realized it was his turn. I started to turn over, but Cinder growled.

"I told you not to move, pet," they said. "He is to keep your thighs spread until I deem you finished."

Mich grunted and spread my thighs again. Cinder started sucking his cock again, rubbing the base as their head bobbed up and down.

"Master," Mich groaned. "I'm going to cum."

Cinder paused for a moment, "You won't until I tell you to. And that won't be until your cock is buried inside of her pussy."

My head fell back on Mich's chest, and I listened as his breaths quickened.

"We need some lube," Cinder said, pulling back.

"Top drawer," Mich groaned.

Cinder nodded and moved across the room, going to a dresser in the corner. They pulled out a bottle of lube, bringing it with them.

"Has anyone ever used your ass before?" Cinder asked.

"A long time ago," Mich said, shivering beneath me. "And I do things to myself."

"Good," Cinder said. "Turn over, ass facing me. Lora beneath you, her legs wrapped around your waist. It'll be easier to fuck you this way."

"Yes, Master," he answered.

In one quick motion, Mich rolled me beneath him. I stared up at him, loving how he looked on top. He was so big, his brawny muscles rippling as he pinned my wrists above my head.

I wrapped my legs around his waist, feeling the tip of his cock rub against me.

He let out a hiss as Cinder applied lube, his eyes closing for a moment.

"So tight," Cinder chuckled. "Mmm. I can't wait to fuck you, slave."

"Please," Mich whimpered.

"Are you ready for your cock to be inside of her?"

"Yes," he gasped.

We stared at each other, losing ourselves as Cinder helped his cock push inside of me. Pleasure ran through me as I gasped, taking every inch of his massive cock.

Cinder moved behind him, gripping his hips. Mich let out a long moan, his head falling forward as he took Cinder inside.

"Good boy," Cinder praised. "Such a good boy. You're doing so well."

Mich's cock pulsed inside of me, and I reached down between us, rubbing my clit.

Cinder pulled out and then thrust forward hard, causing Mich to thrust into me. The three of us moaned together, and Cinder did it again. And again.

I rubbed my clit as Mich fucked me, knowing that our Master was controlling the movements. Knowing that they controlled the rhythm made everything even hotter.

"Please," I groaned. "Fuck I'm going to cum again soon."

"No," Cinder rasped. "Not until I tell you. Both of you will wait until I tell you."

It was going to be torture.

The movements became harder, and Mich cried out, fighting his urge to cum as Cinder fucked him and me.

The three of us fell into a hot rhythm, one that moved faster and harder until Cinder finally cried out.

"Now!"

I gasped as another orgasm crashed into me, this one even more intense than the last. I arched beneath Mich as his knot shoved inside of me, his hot cum filling me. He growled long and low as he took cum and gave it, his body shuddering.

Cinder slowly pulled back and then moved to the side of the bed, collapsing next to me with a happy sigh. Mich knelt his forehead to theirs and gave them a soft kiss.

"Fuck," I gasped. "That was good."

"It was," Cinder said, turning onto their side.

I moved, laying my head on their chest. I was still knotted to Mich, and he slowly lowered himself, his body relaxing on top of mine.

I smiled, the feeling of bliss washing over me.

This week had been absolute hell, but it had ended happily.

Cinder ran their fingers through my hair, kissing the top of my head. "My mates," they murmured.

"What are we doing this weekend?" I asked sleepily.

Mich made a noise, lifting his head. "I told Cinder we should go to my club."

"We should," I said. "I was going to ask you to go out with me, you know. To a club. But then you got hard and naked in the shifting room."

Mich and Cinder both laughed, and I grinned.

"It's not my fault," Mich said. "And I think... I think my rut is broken. I can actually think without my cock."

"Good," Cinder and I both said.

"I mean... I'll go into ruts more often now."

"Oh no," Cinder said blandly. "Oh no, I guess we will have to call in and fuck each other senseless."

We all laughed again. Mich slowly moved, and I gasped as his knot slipped free. He rolled over to the side, groaning. "I'm glad I have a massive bed. We should move in together."

"I've always wanted a house," I said, thinking about it. "With a little picket fence and a cat."

"A cat?" Mich and Cinder both asked.

"Yeah. I could get a kitten and name him Baphomet. Knit my demon circles and drink my tea and be with my mates."

"Is that what your happy place looks like?" Cinder asked.

I bit my lower lip and nodded. "Yes."

"It sounds like a good one," Mich hummed. "Although, I'm more of a dog guy, myself."

"Why not both?" Cinder asked. "I don't know what to do now. I have a regular job, two mates, and my family is safe. What now?"

"I can call my friend Tommy right now, he has a real estate business on the side," Mich said.

I snorted, looking from him to Cinder and then back again. "How about we relax this weekend, and then we figure it out?"

"Sounds like a plan," Cinder sighed happily. "I'm already in my happy place."

"And then work on Monday," I said, scrunching my nose.

"No, no," Cinder hushed. "No talk about work."

I nodded and relaxed again, closing my eyes.

It was Friday, we were off early, I was in the arms of my new mates, and we had the entire weekend ahead of us. For the first time, I couldn't think of one thing to worry about.

"How about an after sex nap?" Mich murmured.

A snore echoed from Cinder, and I fought off a giggle.

Mich snuggled closer to me. I smiled again, thinking about how much everything had changed.

This had been the first week in a life together, one with a future that was much brighter than the past.

## ALFRED- HEAD OF HR

I POURED MYSELF A GLASS OF BONE MARROW WHISKY and downed it, glaring at the mess around me.

While I had been busy dealing with Warts & Claws, Alex had managed to break into one of my facilities and wreck it.

Thirteen omega subjects had been released and were gone.

It was a game, I reminded myself.

Once the omegas were rescued, I wouldn't go after them again. Not unless they were easy to catch.

No, not when they would keep wandering into our offices.

How long would it take until Alex messed up? I had known the witch for centuries, knew how he moved. Knew how he acted.

I had to outsmart him.

"Sir."

I turned to see one of my most loyal agents.

"What do we do?" she asked. "They know about the HR department and security."

"We mix it up," I said, pouring myself another glass. "Let them hire some creatures that aren't spies. Let them think they are safe. And then we will strike again. They will bring in more omegas. Alex always does, even when he doesn't want to. He was the first omega witch, after all."

*clio's creatures*

**Hello Creatures!**

My name is Clio Evans and I am so excited to introduce myself to you! I'm a lover of all things that go bump in the night, fancy peens, coffee, and chocolate.

IF you had the chance to be matched with a monster- what kind would you choose?!

Let me know by joining me on FB and Instagram. I'm a sucker for werewolves to this day.

P.S.

Join my Newsletter by clicking here- I won't spam you, but I will offer you fun rewards for being one of my monster loving creatures.

**Clio's Creature Newsletter**

*thank you*

To Erica Cooke— for being my amazing editor. Thank you for being a wonderful friend and for your support on this monster filled adventure. Also, thank you Morris for always being my first reader. Love you!

## *also by clio evans*